I stopped running before I reached it and stood still, panting for breath, not believing my eyes. Glen backed away and now I could see it quite clearly. It was a *headless body*! Only it wasn't just headless – there was an arm and two legs missing as well. When I looked further along the beach I could see others, some with heads, some heads on their own, some with legs but no arms, some with arms but no legs. It was horrible. I felt sick and strange, as if it were all part of some awful nightmare.

www.**kidsatrandomhouse**.co.uk

The Last Leg

RICHARD KIDD

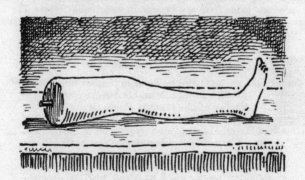

Illustrated by Peter Bailey

CORGI YEARLING BOOKS

For Jamie and Jess

THE LAST LEG
A CORGI YEARLING BOOK 0440 864518

Published in Great Britain by Corgi Books,
an imprint of Random House Children's Books

This edition published 2003

1 3 5 7 9 10 8 6 4 2

Papers used by Random House Children's Books are natural, recyclable
products made from wood grown in sustainable forests. The
manufacturing processes conform to the environmental regulations
of the country of origin.

Set in Century Schoolbook by
Falcon Oast Graphic Art Ltd.

Corgi Books are published by Random House Children's Books,
61–63 Uxbridge Road, London W5 5SA,
a division of The Random House Group Ltd,
in Australia by Random House Australia (Pty) Ltd,
20 Alfred Street, Milsons Point, Sydney, NSW 2061, Australia,
in New Zealand by Random House New Zealand Ltd,
18 Poland Road, Glenfield, Auckland 10, New Zealand,
and in South Africa by Random House (Pty) Ltd,
Endulini, 5A Jubilee Road, Parktown 2193, South Africa

THE RANDOM HOUSE GROUP Limited Reg. No. 954009
www.**kids**at**randomhouse**.co.uk

A CIP catalogue record for this book is available from the British Library.

Printed and bound in Great Britain by
Bookmarque Ltd., Croydon, Surrey

PART ONE

The Misty Isle

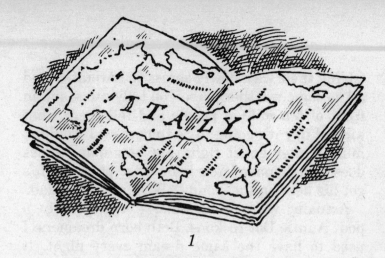

1

The Dream

There are some things you just don't do to people you're supposed to love, like your own children, and one of them is christen them stupid names like Claude.

It was my mum's idea. I was named after her favourite painter, Claude Monet, the guy who painted all those water lilies in France. My dad should have said something. He should have known what it would be like to be out there on the right wing with the ball at your feet and everyone's eyes on you and then someone in the box shouts, '*Claude!*' – but he didn't.

He doesn't say much, my dad, unless it's about the weather. Then there's no stopping him. That's his job. He's a meteorologist, one of those 'behind the scenes' people at the Met Office studying satellite pictures of occluded fronts edging their way slowly across the Atlantic. And all so some weather person on telly can stand in front of ten million people and tell them what kind of day it's going to be tomorrow. I wouldn't mind if they got it right, but how many times does that happen? You know that phrase, 'He's got his head in the clouds'? Well, that's my dad.

Actually, we're quite alike – 'two peas in a pod', Auntie Dot reckons. Both born dreamers. I used to have the same dream every night. It began as a nightmare, but I learnt how to change it. You can do that with practice, so instead of just lying there and having these 'out of control' things happening in your head, you can be ready for them and make other things happen instead. It's like being a film director.

Night dreams are like locked cupboards hidden in some dusty attic waiting for someone to open the door. There's only one key for each dream and only one person owns that key. The dream I'm talking about always begins the same way.

I'm lying on the floor in the living room with the big atlas open at plate 77 – the map of Italy. The map of Italy looks like the bottom half of a leg with the island of Sicily somewhere off the toe, sitting in the sea like a deflated football that's been kicked too hard. You've got the green skin of the coast, the brown muscle of the mountains and the thin red veins of the roads.

You see, that's where we were going just before it happened – a city in Italy called Florence, a third of the way down the leg, tucked behind the kneecap.

Anyway, back to the dream . . . I'm staring at this map looking for a tiny black aeroplane to show me where the airport is when there's a knock at the front door. I'm all alone in the house 'cos Mum's gone to Auntie Dot's to pick up some guide books and Dad's next door talking to our neighbour who's going to water the plants while we're away.

The living-room door's open and through it I can see the oval of dimpled glass in the top half of the front door. There are two heads behind it, both blurred and fragmented, but not so fragmented that I can't make out one is taller than the other and they're both wearing dark blue hats.

I walk into the hallway, but I don't go straight to the door. I stand by the suitcases that are packed and ready with labels tied to their handles. There's another knock at the door, this time on the glass. I can see the pink of the tall one's knuckles. They'd have had to knock because the bell's not working. Dad was going to fix it but said it could wait till we got back.

I'm thinking, Whoever it is will maybe go away. We've got to be at the airport in three hours' time and the last thing we need is some dodgy pair selling religion, or double glazing, or even unbreakable doorbells. But they don't go away. Instead four fat fingers push the letter box open and a man's voice asks, *'Is there anyone at home?'*

I take a step backwards and bump into the suitcases. I'm feeling pretty stupid.

They must have heard me – maybe they can even see me. I know I'm not supposed to open the door to strangers, but I figure Dad's just next door and Mum will be back any minute so I walk to the door and open it.

I'm looking at two policemen – well, a police-*man* and a police*woman*. The policeman is older, with short white hair and a flat peaked cap. The policewoman is much younger, younger than my mum; she's wearing a little domed hat that looks like half a dark blue melon sitting on a black and white gingham tablecloth. They both look slightly surprised to see me, then a two-way radio starts crackling in the policewoman's pocket and a woman's voice starts asking for 'Delta Foxtrot Charlie'. The policeman gives her a quick look of disapproval. I assume he's her boss, because she switches the radio off straight away.

'Does Mr Scott live here?' he asks.

I don't say anything, just nod. All kinds of guilty thoughts are racing through my head. *Could this be something to do with that time six weeks ago when we were playing football on the back field and Alan kicked the ball over the fence and smashed Mr Wervill's greenhouse and we all ran off?* And then it dawned on me – it was my dad they wanted to see. So what had *he* done? Maybe he was being arrested for getting the weather forecast wrong three days in a row?

'Your father . . . is he home?'

'He's just popped next door.'

The policeman hesitates, his brow suddenly creasing into a ploughed field of frowning skin. He glances across the road, where there's a small crowd gathering, and then at the policewoman as if he's asking for her help.

'Do you mind if we come inside?' she asks.

I step aside and let them in. They both stand in the hall staring at the suitcases. I'm half expecting them to say something like, 'Planning a quick getaway, were you?' but they don't. Instead, the policeman removes his cap and tucks it under his left armpit. The policewoman leaves hers on. She smiles at me, but it's only with her mouth, not with her eyes, making me think she'd rather be somewhere else – anywhere except here. I'm beginning to feel the same.

'You can wait in here,' I say, pointing into the living room. They go through and I offer them chairs to sit on. 'No thanks, I'll remain standing,' says the policeman, then turns away from me to

11

check out the back garden. The policewoman perches herself on the very edge of Mum's favourite comfy chair. Her knees are pressed tight together and she's still got that watery smile on her face. She looks down at the atlas. 'Italy,' she says.

I'm thinking, They're playing for time, probably waiting for a back-up team of police marksmen who are at this very moment crawling through the rose bushes in the back garden. 'Shall I go next door and fetch my dad?'

The policewoman looks up at her boss.

'Yes, that might be a good idea,' he says.

I leave the house feeling totally confused. When I get outside Dad's standing at the gate looking at the police car. It's as if his thoughts are written in giant black letters above his head – WHAT ARE THEY DOING HERE? I run down the path towards him and that's when I have to start changing things in the dream because if I don't Dad goes back in the house to talk to the police while I wait outside. And then . . .

Mostly what I make happen is quite simple. Mum appears at the end of the street, not in her old, green Citroën 2CV with the stripy roof, but in something flash and fast like a Porsche or Ferrari. She screeches to a halt alongside the police car. Me and Dad jump in while she revs the engine like mad. *'What about the suitcases?'* I yell.

'*Forget the suitcases!*' shouts Dad. '*Step on it!*'

Mum releases the hand brake and we zoom off, leaving the empty police car and the cheering crowd in a cloud of dust.

Other times, like when I've eaten too much cheese late at night, I dream really wacky endings. Like the time our neighbour held the police off with a water cannon while the three of us escaped in a hot air balloon. Or the time the ivy on the back wall suddenly turned into a carnivorous plant that ate anything dressed in dark blue. It came crashing through the French doors just before Dad arrived. They didn't stand a chance. What a mess!

Sometimes Mum's there and sometimes she isn't. All I know is that when I wake up it's just me and Dad so I try to keep dreaming.

Daydreams are different – they don't just happen, you have to work hard to keep them going. People can see you and because they don't know what's going on in your head they expect you to pay attention and be part of the *real* world – *their* world. It's like being torn in two, being dragged away from somewhere really interesting to dull reality.

That's pretty much how I felt when Dad announced that he had rented a house called Green Shadows on the Isle of Skye.

'*Where?*' I asked.

'The far north-west of Scotland. An island of

13

ancient mountains surrounded by turbulent seas ... igneous intrusions ... unpredictable cyclones ... precipitation within sight.'

I was used to this. 'Not Disney World then?'

'Not this year.'

I shrugged a grudging acceptance. To be honest, I wasn't that bothered about Disney World. An island called Skye sounded custom made for Dad. He needed a break too and if it turned out to be seriously boring I could always dream overtime.

I don't know what I dreamt about that first night on Skye, but I do know that when I woke up it was as if I were still dreaming without even trying.

2

Green Shadows

I was lying in a strange bed in a strange room.
Sunlight was shining through a small window,
which must have been slightly open because
every now and then a whisper of a breeze would
ruffle the curtains and tug teasingly at a spider's
web that spanned one corner.

Without moving my head I moved my eyes,
exploring the room. The walls were papered a
plain creamy white, the colour of old piano keys,
with a few rusty brown damp patches seeping
through in different places. On the window side
they were sloping, so I guessed I was upstairs
under a roof.

At the end of the bed was a battered dressing
table that was too new to be an antique and too
old to be anywhere else except hidden away in
an attic bedroom. On the dressing table was a

lamp made from a bottle that had been covered in tiny seashells.

Hanging on the wall above my head was a small, framed painting with writing on it. I sat up and turned round to look at it. The colours were dark and murky. It seemed to be of a figure on a beach, except the figure didn't have a head. Underneath was written:

Beware all who walk the beach in the
  darkness of the moon
Lest they meet the ghost of the Headless
  Sailor
For their bodies shall be turned to stone,
  cracked by the ice,
Broken by the storms, and worn smooth by
  the sea
To nought but pebbles.

Hmmm, I thought, then lay back down and slowly began remembering.

I remembered getting into the car at home with Dad and Auntie Dot. I was in the back and Auntie Dot was driving. Normally Dad would have driven and I'd have sat beside him, but he'd broken his ankle the week before when he fell out of the tree.

He'd been up there trying to saw off this old dead branch that was threatening to break off and flatten the roses. He couldn't quite reach it

16

with the ladder so he'd sat on the end of the branch nearest the trunk. It was sound theory, but the branch turned out to be even deader than it looked, so the theory didn't hold up and neither did the branch. It snapped off at the trunk and Dad went with it. It was like *Tom and Jerry*. I couldn't stop laughing. Mum would have peed herself. Understandably, it took Dad a while longer to see the funny side, especially with it being so close to our holiday.

We nearly didn't go. That's when Auntie Dot stepped in with the offer to drive. We drove for hours and hours, probably longer than normal because Auntie Dot's what you'd call a *careful* driver. The roads grew narrower and twistier as they threaded their way through massive hills that seemed to suddenly loom out of nowhere. It was beginning to get dark when we passed a fish and chip shop with a sign in the window saying, DEEP FRIED MARS BARS. That was just before Auntie Dot was sick in a lay-by surrounded by black pine trees. She hadn't eaten one – I reckon it was the thought of someone else eating one that had made her sick.

Auntie Dot is Mum's elder sister, but you'd never guess. They're completely different – chalk and cheese. Take food, for instance. Mum would eat anything. I saw her eat an octopus once. It was all chopped up in a bowl of spaghetti and the spaghetti was dark blue 'cos it had been

17

cooked in the octopus ink! Auntie Dot, on the other hand, is very particular about what she eats. She says her body's a shrine and she intends to treat it accordingly.

I must have fallen asleep in the car because I couldn't remember arriving here. I couldn't remember anything after Auntie Dot puking. Someone must have carried me upstairs to bed. I jumped up and pulled back the curtain.

It was as if I'd switched on the telly and suddenly there was this place I'd never seen before right outside my window. The kind of place where no one seems to live. The kind of place they use in car adverts where something red and shiny drives fast along a narrow, winding road until it's just a small cloud of dust in the distance.

There was a field in front of the house – not a flat field like at home but a rough, wild field with lumps and bumps and rocks and thistles. It sloped away towards some trees then fell steeply into the sea, which was glistening in the sunlight as if millions and millions of tiny lights were being switched off and on. In the far distance I could see mountains – not hills, *real* mountains with wispy clouds dragging across their peaks. Or maybe it was smoke? Maybe they were active volcanoes about to erupt?

I found my clothes and pulled them on, all except my socks and trainers. I'd decided in the car on the way up that today's dream was to be an Aborigine and to go walkabout in the Australian outback. They walk for miles and miles across sharp rocks and burning hot sand with nothing on their feet and nothing much on the rest of them either. Maybe later on I'd ditch the T-shirt and paint strange symbols on my body with the juice of crushed leaves and insect blood.

When I stepped outside the bedroom the first thing I noticed was the smell. Not exactly unpleasant, but different and interesting like the smell of other people's food cupboards. It was somewhere between boiled cabbage and beeswax. The paintwork on the stairs was a glossy snot green and the carpet was the colour of purple turnips. This was amazing!

Downstairs there was a conservatory with a giant deep freeze and lots of maps and charts pinned to the walls. The windowsills were covered with smooth, round pebbles, gnarly old seashells and tortured lumps of sun-bleached driftwood. An orange fishing net hung from the ceiling and the floor was a graveyard of abandoned wellies.

I followed the smell of boiled cabbage. Dad was in the kitchen standing over by the sink, staring out of the window. His left leg was encased in plaster from the knee down. Only the tips of his toes poked through.

'Fascinating,' he said.

'What?' I asked.

'Cirrocumulus with altocumulus stratiformis.' He was talking clouds. 'That's not a combination you normally see,' he continued.

'Is there any breakfast?'

'Toast, cereal . . . Wisps of cirrus uncinus. Now that *is* unusual.'

'Toast, please.'

'Cirrus uncinus has a highly characteristic hooked shape. Stop me if I've told you this before.'

'You've told me before.'

'Ice crystals will be forming at the tip where you can see that small tuft of vapour.'

'Is there any jam?'

'On the table. They'll be well over six kilometres high, similar to that layer of cirrocumulus, but much higher than the altocumulus stratiformis, which is probably no more than two or three kilometres high.'

'It's apricot. I hate apricot.'

'There must be considerable wind shear just beneath the generating level.'

'What's that got to do with jam?'

'Pardon?'

'I don't like apricot jam.'

'There's some of Auntie Dot's raspberry in the cupboard.'

This was a fairly typical conversation with

20

Dad. Somehow or other, no matter what it was you were trying to talk about, conversations with Dad always involved the weather. He'd always been like that, but since last summer he seemed to have got worse. He'd thrown himself into his work and stuck his head so far in the clouds that sometimes the only chance of reaching him was by satellite. But I didn't mind: I understood because we were in this together.

'Anything on telly today?' he asked.

That was our private joke – his way of asking me if I was daydreaming.

'Australia,' I said.

'Back for lunch?'

'Dunno.'

'Is it OK to ask what you'll be doing in Australia?'

'Going walkabout like the Aborigines.'

Dad looked back at the clouds. He was quiet, then after a while he said, 'Witchetty grubs. Extremely nutritious. Full of protein. They're like giant maggots about the size of a hen's egg. The Aborigines dig them out of crevices in the rocks, skewer them on the end of a stick and cook them slowly over an open fire.'

He prodded at the floor with one of his crutches and then held the rubber tip over the stove. I could see the giant white maggot squirming on the end, slowly blistering brown like a toasted marshmallow.

'Maybe I'll take a couple of packets of crisps?'

Dad nodded sagely. 'I think there's a beach down there.'

'Great,' I said, briefly remembering the warning above the bed.

'Don't be too late.'

'I won't.'

'And Claude . . .'

'Yes?'

'Shoes.'

'I don't need shoes.'

'Everyone needs shoes.'

'Aborigines don't.'

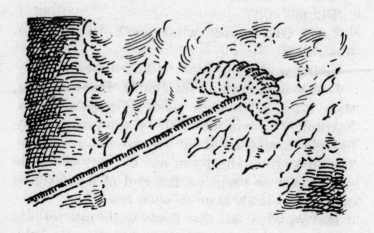

3

The Headless Sailor

Outside, Green Shadows had been painted bubble-gum pink. I hadn't been expecting that. I shut my eyes and opened them slowly, one at a time. It was still bubble-gum pink.

There was a small garden with a jungle of rhubarb plants and a bird table that was covered with an old lobster pot to keep the seagulls off and give the smaller birds a chance. The sunlight was still sparkling on the sea. The sloping field was covered in dew and looked impossibly green, as if every blade of grass had been freshly varnished. I stepped onto it and felt the cool wetness. Was there any wet grass in the Australian outback? Probably not – just jaggy stones and things that lived underneath and bit your feet. I'd read somewhere that Australia had more poisonous creatures than anywhere else in the world.

Scattered across the field were a few dozen sheep and thousands and thousands of black sheep turds. The more you looked, the more there were. Maybe the sheep turds were a plague of killer black scorpions? This was going to be tricky. It was no use rushing things. One sting from those tails and I could forget going walkabout. I'd be dead meat.

I found a stick and sharpened the tip to a point with my penknife. Every self-respecting Aborigine knows there's only one way to deal with killer black scorpions. By the time I met Auntie Dot I'd managed to skewer thirty-seven, but thirty of those had fallen off. The old hard ones that had been baking in the sun for a few days were best. They stayed on.

Auntie Dot was facing the sea. She was sitting cross-legged on a rock at the edge of the field. Her back was poker straight and her hands were resting palm upwards on her knees. 'Ommmmmmm,' she hummed. I didn't reply. I don't think she even knew I was there. I stood with a stick full of dead scorpions hovering inches from her frizzy mop of steely grey hair. She was wearing a baggy white T-shirt and baggy white pants. Actually, most things looked baggy on Auntie Dot. She was majorly skinny, probably because she was so careful about what she ate that she ate hardly anything. Unlike me and Dad, who tended to be on the big side and ate almost anything, except maybe deep fried Mars Bars.

'Ommmmmmm.'

The last of the old dry sheep turds brushed gently against the steely mop. Auntie Dot turned round and stared through her 'no nonsense' black spectacles, first at me and then at the stick. She seemed lost for words.

'Claude,' she said eventually, 'exactly *what* are you doing?'

'Killing scorpions. What does it look like?'

She looked at the stick but didn't seem convinced.

'What are *you* doing?' I asked.

'Yoga,' she replied.

That was something else Auntie Dot did. She was also a bit of a Buddhist on the side. She sat in funny positions and communicated with the cosmos.

'Are they what I think they are?' she asked, still staring at the stick.

I gave the dead scorpions a long hard look and slowly they turned back into sheep turds.

'Your silence speaks volumes,' said Auntie Dot.

I was quite impressed by this: maybe she was telepathic as well and understood about me being an Aborigine for the day.

'Why is it that boys cannot resist the urge to impale things on sticks?'

'They're only sheep turds.'

'Today's sheep droppings may become tomorrow's innocent creatures.'

I let the stick fall to the ground. I'd only just got up and already I was well on the way to becoming a mass murderer.

'You really must try and resist these destructive masculine urges, Claude. They're so negative for your karma.'

I couldn't handle this.

'Where are you going?'

'Down to the sea.'

'Think beautiful thoughts.'

'I'll give it a go,' I said, imagining Auntie Dot being eaten alive by scorpions.

Once you broke through the trees and crossed the road there was a path that led through more trees down to a beach. The air smelled sweet and sour, a mixture of pine needles and seaweed and about as far from the Australian outback as you could possibly get. The beach didn't follow the main coastline, but stretched out at right angles from it on a narrow elbow of land that ended in rocks and a small cliff face. A single small house was perched on top and I could see a faint ribbon of smoke trailing from the chimney. The only other building in sight was a stark, grey church, squatting on the hillside behind the wood.

The tide was low, exposing a thin strip of sand; the rest of the beach was made up of stones –

millions and millions of stones. Not sharp, jaggy ones, but smooth, rounded ones of every shape, size and colour. When I walked on them they felt warm and scrunched together under my bare feet. I kept seeing special ones that were just begging to be picked up. Auntie Dot reckons some stones have their own special energy. She'd go mad if she found this place.

After half an hour of serious stone-collecting my arms were aching under the weight. I piled them up into a miniature mountain, placing a small, curved, white pebble the shape of a crescent moon on the top. Then I walked down to the sea and opened a packet of witchetty grub flavoured crisps.

It was about then that I spotted the footprints in the sand, a man and a dog. Probably a different tribe. Perhaps a hunting party. I was still inspecting them when the dog appeared from nowhere. He was an old black and white collie with one white eye and a friendly face. I sat very still and held out my hand. He lowered his head, sniffed my hand and dropped a pebble he'd been carrying in his mouth. Then he jumped back and began running round and round in circles, stopping every now and then to stare at the pebble then at me. I guessed he wanted me to throw it so I did, and seconds later he was back for more. This went on for ages. It was like having a boomerang until someone whistled and the dog ran off in the direction of the little house on the cliff.

I stayed for a while longer, trying to tune back into my Aboriginal dream time, but I'd lost it, so I set off back down the beach towards the pine trees and the path that led up the hill to Green Shadows. It was midday and there wasn't a breath of wind. The altocumulus stratiformis was now a thick blanket blotting out the sun. The tide was turning and the sea was eerily calm, like a mirror with no reflection. There were no birds, just the slow, steady lapping of the exhausted waves. It was the same beach I'd walked along earlier in the morning but now it felt completely different. It was as if everything had stopped and was waiting to start again.

I didn't notice the black boat at first, probably because it was floating in shallow water next to some black rocks. And when I did I didn't notice the dark figure stooped over it until it moved. He had his back to me and seemed to be looking for something in the bottom of the boat.

'Claude! Claude!'

I turned round and saw Auntie Dot waving madly. When I turned back the figure had vanished.

4

Angel of the Islands

'You are what you eat,' said Auntie Dot at breakfast the next morning.

'That's food for thought,' muttered Dad, who was standing over the cooker frying bacon.

'Does that mean we're pigs?' I asked.

'Not exactly,' said Auntie Dot in a superior kind of way, 'but quite apart from the fact that the complex protein structure of meat is difficult for your body to digest, a life has been sacrificed to satisfy your appetite.'

Dad hung his head and stared thoughtfully into the frying pan. I took a defiant bite of my bacon sandwich.

'What about plants?' I asked.

'Plants are different, they don't have feelings,' retorted Auntie Dot defensively.

'Some plants grow faster when you play them

music. If they like music they must have feelings.'

Auntie Dot stared thoughtfully at the banana on her plate. 'That's not the same. Fruit is meant to be eaten.'

'So are pigs,' I said.

'I can see my words are falling on stony ground,' she said, grimly peeling the banana.

'I bet you'd eat bacon if you had to,' I said.

'No I wouldn't.'

'Not even if you were starving?'

'Not even then.'

'You mean you'd rather die than eat a bacon buttie?'

'I have my principles.'

'I can't imagine how anyone could refuse a bacon buttie. Just the smell of one makes me hungry. I could eat them till they come out my ears.'

'That, Claude, is because you are a born carnivore who was reared on the taste of blood.'

'You make me sound like some vampire!'

'Vampires have an excuse. They *need* blood.'

'I need bacon!'

Auntie Dot took her naked banana and left the room.

'What's up with her?' I asked.

'We seem to be on the edge of a slow-moving anticyclone,' said Dad. 'There's a deep depression over the Azores.'

'That explains things then,' I said sarcastically.

Dad hobbled off to find Auntie Dot so I took my buttie and went outside. The old collie dog I'd met on the beach was waiting on the other side of the garden gate. He must have smelled the bacon 'cos his long pink tongue was hanging out and he was whining pleadingly. I gave him what was left, which meant we were now the best of mates. We walked across the field, down through the trees and onto the beach. The priority of the day was to find the Headless Sailor, or at least see if his boat was still there.

It was, exactly where I'd seen it yesterday afternoon except the tide was way out and it was high and dry on the pebbles. There was no sign of any ghost and I decided that if this was a ghost boat I'd be able to walk straight through it, but I smelled it before I got close enough to touch it. That convinced me it was real. It seemed pretty unlikely that a ghost boat would stink of dead fish.

It was about four metres long and made of wood that had been tarred black and then bleached by the sun. On the prow someone had painted the words ANGEL OF THE ISLANDS. I approached it slowly, only half expecting to find a detached head rolling round in the bottom, staring into space. Instead there were ordinary things like coils of rope, fishing lines, rusty tin

31

cans and an ancient pair of oars, the handles of which had been worn smooth and shiny with use.

The pebbles behind me suddenly scrunched and the dog started barking. I turned round and saw an old man walking down the beach towards me. The dog ran up to greet him and he patted it on the head. He was wearing dark blue trousers that looked as though he'd been dropped into them from somewhere high up, because the waistband was tied round his chest with a piece of string and the bottoms ended halfway down his shins. On his feet he had sawn-off black wellies. He wore an old grey shirt and an old grey cap. His hands were huge and gnarly with fingers like thick brown sausages; his face a weather-beaten brown covered in a frost of white bristles. When he got closer I could see his crinkly eyes were a bright shiny blue.

'You've met Glen then?' he said, nodding at the dog. 'My name's Roderick, but everyone calls me Roddy. Everyone, that is, except my sister. She still calls me Roderick.'

'Mine's Claude.'

'Claude,' he repeated slowly with a smile on his face. 'That's a nice name.' And the way he said it, it *did* sound nice.

'Is that your house on top of the cliff?' I asked.

'Aye, that's me.'

'And is this your boat?'

32

'Indeed it is.'

'I saw you yesterday. I thought you were the Headless Sailor.'

The old man laughed. 'And who's been filling your head with all that nonsense?' he asked.

'I read about it in the house.'

'The pink house?'

'Yes, I'm staying there with my dad and aunt.'

'Is that so,' he said thoughtfully, and for an awful moment I thought he was going to ask about my mum.

'Is it true? Is there really a ghost?' I blurted.

'There was a body,' he said, sitting down on the back of the boat. 'It was me that found it. There'd been a terrible storm and a boat had gone down in the Black Skerries. It wasn't until a few days later that he was washed up. We buried him in the churchyard, without the head. That was never found.'

'My dad doesn't believe in ghosts,' I said.

'No one believes in ghosts until they've seen one.'

'Have you seen one? Have you seen the Headless Sailor?'

He smiled gently, in the way old people are really good at, and rubbed the white bristles on his chin with his sausage fingers. 'Let's just say I don't disbelieve in ghosts.' He reached down into the boat and lifted out a red plastic bucket. 'Lugworms,' he said. 'It's low tide and I

33

came down to dig for lugworms, for the fishing.'

'Can I help?' I asked.

'If you've a mind to.'

'Yes please.'

'Then we'll fetch the gripe.'

The gripe turned out to be a big garden fork that was kept in a little corrugated iron shed painted green and hidden behind the rocks on the edge of the wood. We walked down to the sea across the flat wet sand, which was strewn with what looked like small portions of spaghetti, but were, in fact, worm casts. Roddy began digging with the gripe and soon the bucket was a seething mass of lugworms. They were seriously disgusting! The best bit was pulling them out of the wet sand as they tried to escape. Sometimes they'd snap in two and both bits would keep wriggling, with dark red guts hanging out. My fingers were bright yellow.

'That's the iodine from the worms,' explained Roddy. 'You'll need to wash your hands.'

'What do you catch with them?' I asked.

'That depends.'

'On what?'

'On what's biting,' he said with another gentle smile. 'Codling, haddock, whiting – perhaps nothing – but if it stays calm there'll be mackerel for sure.'

'I've never eaten mackerel.'

'A fresh mackerel is the finest eating the sea

has to offer and it's a fighter. A shoal of mackerel feeding on the surface will make the sea boil. It's not unusual to catch two on the same hook. And if you've more than one hook they'll near pull your arm off before you land them.'

I was thinking about this, trying to imagine how it felt.

'You've never been fishing?' he asked.

'No.'

'Would you like to try?'

'Yes!'

'Well, if it's all right with your father and your aunt in the pink house, then you can come out this evening. Them that digs the bait gets to catch the fish.'

'Really?'

'Aye, the tide'll be high round six and that's when the mackerel will be biting.'

'I'll be there.'

5

The Fairy Folk

We were still on the edge of a slow-moving anti-cyclone. The pink house was bathed in green shadows. Auntie Dot had gone castle spotting. Dad was sitting in the garden looking at the sun through a piece of smoked glass, his white, plastered leg cooling in the shade of the rhubarb plants. 'Sun spots,' he said. 'Stop me if I've told you this before . . .'

'You've told me before.'

'. . . but these violent solar eruptions have a profound effect upon our weather.'

'Anything happening?' I asked, mildly curious.

'Possibly,' lowering his grey monocle and blinking his eyes.

'Can I go fishing later on?'

'Your fingers are yellow.'

'It's the iodine from the worms.'

'Fascinating.'

I took this for a 'yes' and at six o 'clock met Roddy on the beach. The tide was high and the *Angel of the Islands* was half in and half out of the water. Roddy took a cork from his pocket and pushed it hard into a hole in the bottom of the boat. 'We'll be needing that if we're to stay afloat.' I must have looked concerned. 'Don't worry,' he laughed. 'My *Angel* hasn't sunk yet. She's an old lady and her timbers aren't as watertight as they once were, but she'll see us safe ashore.'

I sat at the back with my feet amongst the fishing tackle. Roddy pushed the boat out then clambered in, his sawn-off wellies only just managing to keep his feet dry. He sat down in the middle and began rowing slowly, dipping the oars in the water and pulling them back with long, smooth strokes that left nothing but tiny ripples where they broke the surface. The sea was a glassy grey mirror and I felt like a fly crawling across it. Soon we were far from the shore. I could see the pink dot of Green Shadows way up on the hill and wondered what Dad was doing.

'We'll try our luck here,' said Roddy, lifting the oars out of the water and back into the boat. He dropped the anchor over the side, narrowly missing a passing jellyfish, then he unwound the fishing lines, reached over for the red plastic

37

bucket and impaled two black lugworms on the barbed hooks.

We lowered the lines over the side until the weight at the end hit the bottom and the lines went slack, then we pulled them up a little and waited. It was Roddy who got the first bite. He gave the line a sharp tug and began pulling it in. I leant over the side and watched as the pale shape of the fish grew larger and larger as it was hauled unwillingly from the murky dark to the bright surface: a writhing, beady-eyed haddock that fell limply on the tarred planks, shuddering and twitching as it stared uncomprehendingly at the sky.

I couldn't help thinking about Auntie Dot and what she'd said the day before. I told myself that fish didn't feel pain the way we do, that their brains weren't developed enough to understand what was happening. But then why did they pull so hard trying to get free of the hook? A solitary seagull floating nearby swam closer in the hope of an easy meal. I remembered how seagulls were supposed to peck out the eyes of ship-wrecked sailors. I stared at the long yellow beak tipped with a hook of scarlet like a drop of blood. The eyes were mean and cruel. Seagulls weren't worried about causing pain. It was all about survival. They were hunters, but then so was the haddock. The haddock had to eat something – probably smaller fish, which in turn ate even smaller fish. Everything was eating something else.

We caught four more before we hit the shoal of mackerel. I hadn't understood what Roddy meant by the sea 'boiling' until I saw it happen. They were feeding on the surface, snapping at tiny sand eels. Even the seagull flew off, probably worried that its feet would be next. Roddy didn't bother with the worms but quickly tied white feathers to the hooks. They'd barely broken the surface when the mackerel bit. These fish weren't like the haddock; they were sleeker, more pointed, built for speed. They were fighters and a few even tore free of the hook and swam to freedom, but most landed up in the boat. In less than ten minutes the *Angel of the Islands* was carpeted in row upon row of glistening green and black stripes, studded with staring eyes. The lone seagull was back, this time with a few friends. Word had got round.

'That's enough,' said Roddy, winding in his line for the last time.

'But they're still biting,' I said.

'So they are. But they'll be biting again to-morrow and the day after that and it's a wise man who takes what he needs and not what he can.'

Roddy gutted the fish, throwing handfuls of the dark red and orange intestines to the attentive gulls, who tossed back their heads and swallowed them whole. When we reached the shore there was a breeze blowing from the west and a faint ribbon of smoke was trailing from the chimney of Roddy's croft on the cliff. You could smell it – a rich, earthy smell, almost sweet. There was a distant clatter like someone banging a tin bucket with a stick. I looked towards the white house and saw the stooped figure of an old woman dressed in black.

'Aye, that'll be Katie feeding the hens,' mused Roddy.

'Is that your sister?'

'It is. We've lived in the same house for over eighty years, except during the war. During the war I was overseas.'

'Whereabouts?'

'In Italy, mostly.'

'Did you have to kill anyone?'

Roddy didn't seem to want to answer and busied himself with mooring the boat.

'Did anyone try and kill you?'

'Lots of people,' he laughed. 'But without much success. Now let's take these fish and drop the tackle off at the wee shed.'

We walked over the rocks to the edge of the wood where the little green hut stood almost invisible in the shadows. The sun was low in the sky now and the wood seemed to have closed in, become denser, bathed in a dark green light. Little silver birch trees and hazel trees grew side by side on a dense carpet of moss. Roddy opened the door.

'Don't you bother locking it?' I asked.

'Locks are only to keep honest men out and honest men are quite welcome to look inside. Besides, I wouldn't want to offend the small dark people.'

'Who?'

'The fairy folk.'

'Do you believe in fairies?'

'I do.'

'Does that mean you've seen them?'

'It does.'

'What are they like?'

'Small and dark skinned. They wear clothes like you and me, only more old fashioned.'

'Where do they live?'

'Underground mostly, although some live in the sky and others in the sea. They're the little blue men, the fallen angels.' A gust of wind suddenly shook the leaves of the hazel trees and rattled the door of the shed. 'It's wise to make friends with the small dark people. I leave the door open, in case they want to borrow the gripe or some fishing line. Better it be borrowed than stolen.'

'How do you know when they've borrowed something?'

'Because it's always there when I come back, but not always in the same place.'

41

Inside the shed there was a single wooden chair and a little worktop covered with tins and glass jars, stuffed full of things like feathers and hooks, rusty nails and neat little bundles of coloured string. Various tools were leaning against the wall and on a shelf high up stood a bottle of whisky and a brown paper bag. Roddy reached up and lifted it down. 'My medicine,' he said, taking a swig. 'Just a wee dram or two in the evenings. It's good for the constitution, but best you don't mention it to my sister.'

'I won't.'

'She's very religious and doesn't approve.' He took another nip, wiped his stubbly mouth on the sleeve of his shirt and reached up for the brown paper bag. 'Would you like a peppermint?'

'Thanks.'

'I'll have one too,' he said with a wink. 'And now I'm thinking you'll be needing fresh potatoes to go with that mackerel and maybe a sprig of mint.'

'That would be great.'

'Then we'll walk up to the house and you can say hello to Katie.'

We walked along the beach carrying the fish in a bucket. Glen met us halfway, barking excitedly, then ran off ahead. The sky in the west was starting to turn pink and all around the brightness of the blue was deepening, but there was still plenty of light. It really didn't get dark till way after midnight and it was only eight o'clock. At the end of the beach a path led up the hillside to the top of the promontory where Roddy's house stood.

It was small, squat and built of stones painted white. The roof was thatch, held in place with fishing net from which dangled rocks tied to lengths of rope. There were two small windows and a single small door painted blue. The ground seemed to be mostly solid rock strewn with black plastic buckets of red geraniums and dark green herbs. Over by the cliff edge there was a small fenced off area that had been planted with vegetables.

When I first stepped inside I could hardly see, it was that dark. It was like being underground in a cave. Not that it was cold, or damp, or dirty. Far from it. It was the cosiest room I'd ever been in. The floor seemed to be solid rock scattered with odd bits of carpet. The walls were completely covered with pictures from old magazines and Christmas cards that had been pasted over the stone instead of wallpaper. There was a cross above the door and a picture of Jesus above the fireplace. The whole room was filled with the sweet, earthy smell of smoke from the peat fire smouldering in the hearth. A little grey-haired lady with skin as soft and wrinkled as an overripe grape came through from the other room. She was dressed in black and was

43

wiping her hands on a faded tartan tea towel.

'So the fishermen have returned from the sea,' she said with a friendly twinkle in her eyes.

'Aye, this is Claude. Claude, this is Katie.'

'Pleased to meet you,' I said.

'Likewise, I'm sure,' she said. 'And now, Roderick Fraser, will you kindly remove that bucket of smelly fish from the living-room floor and put it outside where it belongs.'

Roddy nodded and silently obeyed.

'You'll be hungry after being at sea,' she said.

'A bit,' I replied.

'And thirsty too no doubt,' she added, staring pointedly at Roddy.

'I'm going to lift some potatoes for Claude,' he said in retreat.

'Sit yourself down, Claude. I'll make a cup of tea and you'll have a cheese scone.'

I wasn't about to argue. The tea tasted of peat, but the scone was delicious.

They both stepped outside to say goodbye.

'Will you be fishing tomorrow?' I asked hopefully.

'Not tomorrow,' said Roddy.

'Tomorrow is the Sabbath,' said Katie solemnly. 'The day our Lord rested and all good Christians should do the same.'

'Sorry, I forgot.'

'Are you a good Christian, Claude?'

'I think so,' I said rather too hesitantly, then

added, 'My dad's a meteorologist and my Auntie Dot's a Buddhist.'

I could see this didn't go down too well with Katie Fraser.

'I'll be taking the boat out on Tuesday morning,' said Roddy, trying hard not to laugh. 'If you've a mind to, I could use an extra pair of hands.'

'I'll be there.'

'Eight o'clock sharp then.'

You could see the pink house from Roddy's croft and I noticed there was a light on in the kitchen. It took a while to get back, what with having to carry the fish and potatoes. Roddy said we should have them for breakfast, but I wasn't sure about that.

The back door was open. I left the fish and potatoes outside and walked through to the kitchen. There was an empty bottle of wine, a lit candle and a rhubarb crumble on the table. Dad and Auntie Dot were staring into each other's eyes and holding hands. I wanted to be somewhere else. Auntie Dot dropped Dad's hand and jumped out of her chair. She stared at me as if I'd just landed from Mars.

'You're covered in blood!' she screamed.

6

Before the Storm

That night I had the same old dream – the map of Italy, the police . . . the works. But when I reached the part where I was supposed to step in as director everything went haywire. I thought the 'carnivorous ivy' dream was weird but this was something else. The police were tied to the comfy chairs and wrapped in fishing net, with Auntie Dot force-feeding them deep fried Mars Bars. The living-room floor was covered in a shoal of man-eating mackerel, who were chewing toes, and the air was full of screeching seagulls trying to peck everyone's eyes out. Roddy was barring the door with his gripe, Dad was stomping on his plaster leg and Katie was standing in the corner on a pulpit bashing a huge black Bible up and down. Even the small dark people were there, staring through the

46

window and laughing. Everyone was there . . . everyone except Mum.

When I woke up I was covered in sweat with half the bedclothes on the floor and the other half wrapped round me like some half-dressed Egyptian mummy. The seagulls in my dream were still screeching. I rolled out of bed, hopped over to the window and pulled back the curtains in time to see the last of the mackerel being greedily devoured.

I dragged myself downstairs and into the kitchen. Auntie Dot was over by the sink, singing as she wrung the soapy water from my spotless jeans.

'Good morning, Claude,' she chirped.

'Morning,' I yawned.

'Sleep well?'

'Not sure.'

'Why's that?'

'I was asleep.'

Auntie Dot looked as though she might comment on this, but thought better of it and instead gave me the kind of tight-lipped smile you give a baby who's just been sick on your lap.

'Where's Dad?'

'Still asleep, bless him.'

Bless him! Was that something else Buddhists did? Go around blessing other people's dads without being asked. She marched out of the room holding my dripping jeans at arm's length.

I sat at the table and lowered my head into a bowl of cornflakes.

Dad didn't emerge until midday. Auntie Dot drove us to a ruined castle, perched on some rocks overlooking the sea, and while Auntie Dot and I did the tourist bit Dad sat in the car and tried to tune in to the shipping forecast. It had started to rain and the castle was seriously bleak. When we got back to the car Dad informed us that the high pressure area in the Atlantic and the low pressure area over Iceland had formed a symmetrical pattern that was being crossed by the remnants of a weak occluded front. So much for Sunday.

Monday wasn't much better, but during the night the low pressure area was pushed west over Greenland and the high pressure area moved north and east, settling over Scotland. The occluded front fizzled out altogether so on Tuesday morning the sun was shining again.

Roddy was already on the beach, bailing out rainwater from the *Angel of the Islands* with a rusty tin can. The lines were in the boat and the bucket was full of worms. I was back on holiday. I told him about the gulls getting the mackerel and he just laughed.

We went out fishing every day. We'd nearly always catch enough for a meal and what was left over Roddy would take home and put in a barrel of salt in order to preserve it for the winter when the sea was too rough to take the boat out. Back in the pink house Dad was becoming a seafood master chef and Auntie Dot could get the fish blood out of a pair of jeans faster than you could say 'mackerel'.

In the quiet times at sea Roddy would tell me stories. That was one of the best things about being out there. I'd just sit in the back of the boat listening and dreaming of the giant Hag of the Ridges, who flew over Skye every winter to wash her linen in a whirlpool and then hang it out to dry on the mountaintops. Weathermen thought it was snow, but actually it was the hag's giant knickers! About the mermaids that swim in the Black Skerries and the Norse god, Oegir, who lifts his head from the waves to call up storms. About the man who sailed from Skye to Raasay to rid the island of witches. And how, when he was halfway across, the sea suddenly turned black with cats that had swum out from Raasay. And how they climbed out of the water and covered his boat until it sank beneath the waves.

On the Friday Roddy and I went out at lunchtime but we didn't stay out for long. A north-west wind began to blow across the sea and the smooth grey mirror was suddenly shattered into a million jagged fragments. There were black clouds building up over Raasay. The kind of black clouds that usually mean business.

Roddy lifted the oars and sniffed the air.

'There's a storm brewing,' he said, squinting his eyes almost shut.

'Should we be getting back?' I asked as the waves began to jostle the boat.

'Perhaps that would be wise,' he said, nodding slowly.

I sat in the back looking towards the shore, but I couldn't see the pink house. The boat suddenly seemed vulnerable, as if the sea had woken up after a long sleep and was irritated with us being there. Waves began breaking over the prow and the salty spray thrashed against the bottom of the boat, soaking us from head to foot. I began to feel a bit scared, but Roddy looked quite calm and I managed to distract myself thinking of all those fish swimming beneath us, wondering whether they could sense the approaching storm.

It took us much longer to row back, and by the time we reached the shore we were both cold and wet. We dragged the *Angel of the Islands* up onto the pebbles. Roddy tied her to her mooring on the rocks then stood for a while gazing out to sea, where the Isle of Raasay had completely changed colour from a pale green to a dark, brooding blue.

'Aye, it'll not be long in coming,' he mused. 'We'll be in for a bad night. I'd best go and batten down the hatches at home.'

'Suppose so,' I said, kicking at the pebbles.

'Katie's making cheese scones. Would you like one?'

We sat in semi darkness, huddled round the peat fire with the wind moaning down the chimney. Roddy told me the story of the fairy cows, the cows that belonged to the blue men in the sea. How every day the cows would walk out of the waves and up onto the land to graze and at night they'd return to the sea. And how one night a young boy heard the blue men calling in their cows. How he gathered a handful of soil from a mole hill and another from the church-yard and ran down to the water's edge. The fairy cows were just about to enter the sea when he threw the soil between them and the waves. The fairy cows could not cross and so they remained on Skye for ever.

Katie came in with warm scones and a jug of fresh milk. 'Stuff and nonsense,' she said.

'It is not,' said Roddy defensively.

'It is so.'

'Then why do you always see cows on the beach staring out to sea?'

'They go on the beach to eat the seaweed.'

'So they do,' agreed Roddy, 'but they still stare out to sea.'

'Pah!' said Katie, rising to her feet and bustling out of the room. She paused by the kitchen door. 'I expect you've been filling

51

the boy's head full of fairies and ghosts and other such pagan tittle-tattle.' Roddy looked up but remained silent. 'Pah!' she repeated and left the room.

'She doesn't like hearing the stories,' whispered Roddy. 'And it's not because she doesn't believe them. It's because she does. Now, would you like a cabbage to take back with you? It would be a shame to arrive home empty handed.'

Cabbage wasn't my favourite vegetable, but I didn't want to offend Roddy. It was the thought that counted. We walked to the edge of the cliff, where the rock gave way to rich peaty soil and where Roddy had a small vegetable patch. He cut the thick stem of the cabbage with an old rusty knife and handed it to me. It was round and dense and a lot heavier than it looked.

'Best be getting back then,' I said. 'I'll see you later.'

'You will.'

By the time I reached the end of the beach the Isle of Raasay had totally disappeared, swallowed by hungry black clouds that were moving ever closer. The wind had found a voice and the sea was shaking itself like a wet dog. Seagulls were wheeling overhead looking for eyes to peck out. It was wild.

I clutched the cabbage to my chest and thought of the Headless Sailor. Did ghosts come out in the afternoon? Or did they have to wait until after dark? There was a brown cow by the water's edge, staring into the face of the storm. I started running and didn't stop until I reached Green Shadows.

Dad was listening to the radio. *'Storm Force Ten forecast for sea areas Rockall, Malin and Hebrides.'*

'Storm Force Ten!' exclaimed Dad excitedly. 'I knew it. I've been observing the development of this storm since its humble beginning as a mere blip on a polar front.'

'Really?' said Auntie Dot, sounding seriously impressed.

'It was the slow development of the warm and cold fronts over Tuesday and Wednesday with the closed circular wind pattern that was the first clue. Then the slow build-up of extensive cloud cover on Thursday, stratiform on the warm front and convective on the cold front . . . Well, that was a dead giveaway!'

I dumped the cabbage on the kitchen table. No one seemed to notice. The first splatters of rain tapped at the kitchen window.

'And then, that strong updraught in the cumulonimbus early this morning could mean only one thing.' Auntie Dot was nodding enthusiastically. 'A squall front with the consequent uplift triggering severe instability,' continued Dad. He was on a roll.

'It's raining,' I said.

'New convective cells are obviously forming ahead of the main storm establishing a large-scale organized air flow. If we're really lucky this could be a Supercell Storm!'

'What happens then?' asked Auntie Dot, her eyes wide with anticipation.

'The house blows away,' I suggested.

'The whole system develops into a single, giant, organized circulation,' said Dad, going all glassy eyed.

'Ooooh,' sighed Auntie Dot in ecstasy.

I gave the cabbage a nudge and they both turned round.

'Claude. A cabbage. Is that for me?'

I looked at the cabbage, then I looked back at Auntie Dot. I swear there were tears in her eyes. I had no idea that cabbages could have that effect on people.

After the Storm

The centre of the storm passed over us on Friday night. It was like being inside a washing machine when it suddenly switches to fast spin. I lay in bed listening to the wind and the rain buffeting the house. It wasn't a steady wind, it came in gusts. You could hear it howling like some wild animal on the loose, rushing towards you, then *WHAM!* the whole house seemed to move. Things on the dressing table would start rattling, the curtains would rustle even though the windows were closed, and when it eased off the creaking and groaning would start as if poor old Green Shadows were bracing herself for the next onslaught.

I thought about Katie and Roddy in their little stone croft. If it was bad here it must be twice as bad on that cliff top. I climbed out of bed and pulled back the curtain to see if I could see them. It was like looking into a bucket of black paint that someone was stirring very fast. Every twelve seconds the lighthouse on Raasay flashed a brief pinprick of light, casting a beam that for a split second shone across a sea that was being ripped wide open. The rain thrashed against the window like a handful of gravel and the blackness returned.

I went back to bed and sometime in the early hours fell fast asleep. I had the dream again, except this time when the police came to our door they were soaking wet. They said their boat had sunk and they needed shelter; there were more of them out there. Mum wrapped them in warm blankets and gave them mugs of hot chocolate. Me and Dad put on our wellies and went into the garage to launch the lifeboat, but when we opened the door the sea rushed in. We swam round for a bit until we found the stairs. We climbed up to the attic and through a skylight onto the roof. Mum was already there with the Headless Sailor, cooking bacon on the chimney pot. We sat down beside her. The whole roof was covered with dark blue policemen, who kept slipping off and falling into the water. It was then that the sharks arrived.

When I woke up it was light, that pale watery light you get after a storm. The wind was still blowing but nothing like the night before. I couldn't be bothered with bacon, not after I'd seen what the sharks had done. Auntie Dot gave me a banana and I left for the beach. Halfway across the field I met Glen. He was barking like crazy, racing ahead then stopping and barking again. Something was up.

The tide was right out but instead of being flat calm the sea was angry and irritable. It had been up all night. Glen ran over the rocks and down to the sand. Something was missing. Roddy's boat! I walked over to the mooring and found the rope with a frayed and tattered end lying on the rocks. Then I saw it, lying on its back with the sides all smashed in. The storm must have broken the mooring rope and tossed it like a matchbox onto the rocks. What was Roddy going to say? How was I going to tell him? Then I saw the footprints in the sand and I knew I didn't have to tell him. He already knew and I could guess where I'd find him.

The door of the little green hut was wide open and Roddy was sitting on his chair with his hands on his knees staring at an empty whisky bottle. I stopped a few metres from the door and stood in silence. Slowly he turned round to face me. The twinkle in his eyes had gone and he looked about a hundred years old.

'Claude,' he said.

'Hi.'

'I'm afraid there'll be no more fishing for a while.'

'I know.'

'Then you've seen her?'

'Yes.'

'I must be getting old. I should have known the storm was going to be a bad one. I should have dragged her right out of the water.'

'Can she be repaired?'

'Too old. Too badly damaged.'

'I'm sorry.'

'Ach, it's one of those things.'

'Will you get a new boat?'

'No, I shouldn't think so.'

'But the fish . . . How will you catch fish?'

'There's enough salted to see us through the winter and I'm thinking there'll not be many more winters to worry about.'

I felt like crying, but didn't. 'Does Katie know?' I asked.

'No,' he said, rising unsteadily to his feet. 'I suppose I'd better go and tell her.'

'I'll come with you if you like.'

'Yes. She'd appreciate that.'

Roddy staggered out of the hut, leaving the door wide open.

'Do you want me to close it?' I asked.

'No, I'd best leave it open for the little dark people. They can take what they want. I must have offended them in some way. Otherwise why would they not have looked after my boat?'

There was no answer to that.

Glen started barking. He was down on the beach. He didn't seem to want to come into the wood. By the time we'd scrambled over the rocks he was going berserk. Perhaps it was the wind, the different smells – who knows? He raced along the edge of the sea, leaving wet paw prints in the sand that vanished with the sweep of each new wave. He must have been fifty metres ahead when he stopped and began sniffing at something. He turned back towards us, but instead of barking he was whining.

'What's that Glen's found?' asked Roddy.

'I don't know,' I said, squinting my eyes.

I ran ahead. The wind was blowing spray from the tops of the waves and the sunlight was shining through, making rainbows. You could smell the sourness of the seaweed that the storm had dragged up from the sea bed and dumped on the beach. I thought that was what Glen was sniffing at, but it wasn't; it was something tangled amongst the seaweed.

I stopped running before I reached it and stood still, panting for breath, not believing my eyes. Glen backed away and now I could see it quite clearly. It was a *headless body*! Only it wasn't just headless – there was an arm and two legs missing as well. When I looked further along the beach I could see others, some with

59

heads, some heads on their own, some with legs but no arms, some with arms but no legs. It was horrible. I felt sick and strange, as if it were all part of some awful nightmare.

I turned to Roddy but I couldn't speak. He'd stopped about ten metres behind me. He'd seen them too. His mouth was hanging open and he was clutching his chest as if he couldn't breathe. Glen started barking again as a wave washed another body ashore. It was the top half of a woman. Her arms were stiff as if rigor mortis had already set in. The wave receded and her face rolled towards me. She was smiling and there was something else weird: she was completely bald and naked – they all were. *They were dummies!* Shop-window mannequins. I let out a huge sigh of relief, shook my head and turned back to Roddy.

'It's not what you think. They're not real. They're dummies.'

'Dummies?' repeated Roddy.

'Shop-window mannequins that people use to display clothes. They must come apart, that's why they're all in bits. There must be dozens of them.'

'Thank the Lord. I thought . . .'

'So did I. But where did they come from?'

'A cargo ship,' mused Roddy. 'Perhaps they broke loose in the storm.'

And then I had an idea. 'Roddy, if we find

them on the beach that's like salvage. That means they're ours.'

'That is so.'

'Well, they must be worth something. They're not that badly damaged.'

'You may be right.'

'If we collect them we could sell them, or maybe whoever they belong to would give us a reward for finding them. We might make enough money to buy a new boat!'

Roddy smiled. 'That's a kind thought. And I suppose it's an ill wind that blows no good.'

We began dragging the dismembered mannequins out of the water, making a grotesque pile at the far end of the beach beneath the cliff. It was a grim task. I counted twenty-eight arms, thirty-one legs, thirteen torsos and fourteen heads. They were all hollow, made from pink fibreglass, which explained why they didn't sink and instead were washed ashore.

I arranged all the heads in a single line with their faces looking out to sea. It looked surreal, especially with all the faces being the same – a lady with high cheekbones, large blue eyes and dark red lips set in a gentle smile. She looked strangely content; they all did. I counted them again . . . thirteen: there was one missing. Roddy was sitting on a rock cradling the fourteenth head in his lap, staring into her face.

61

'If she'd had black curls . . .' he said to himself.
'Pardon?'

'If only . . .' he began, but stopped and sighed.

I looked at the head. It was different from the others. It had a more thoughtful expression and even though it was larger than the others, slightly larger than life size, it somehow looked more realistic.

'What's wrong?' I asked. And it was then that Roddy told me his story. The story of the real *Angel of the Islands*.

It began towards the end of the war, when Roddy was captured by the Germans in Italy. As the Germans retreated north they took some prisoners with them. Roddy was one of those, but he managed to escape by jumping from a train somewhere north of Florence. He walked south through the mountains, sticking to the smallest roads and sleeping rough under hedges and in barns, hoping to meet up with the American army, which had landed in the south and was advancing northwards.

One morning, somewhere in the countryside near Florence, he was in a barn helping himself to some eggs when he was discovered by the daughter of an Italian farmer. Her name was Angelina. They fell in love and Angelina and her family hid Roddy until the Americans had liberated Italy. When the war was over they married and Roddy took his bride back to the Isle of Skye.

For a while they lived happily. Angelina was used to the simple life, but Roddy's sister, Katie, was not used to having another woman in the house. Katie offered to leave but after the war times were particularly hard and Roddy wouldn't hear of it. Things went from bad to worse. Angelina began to feel homesick. She missed Italy, especially the Italian sunshine. Skye can be a bleak and desolate place in winter – it's not for nothing that it's known as the Misty Isle.

Angelina would spend all day on the beach, staring out to sea, south towards her homeland. The winter nights were long and dark and the days often shrouded in mist. One winter's night Roddy returned home to find Angelina had gone. She'd packed her bag and left for Italy with barely enough money to reach Glasgow. Roddy went after her, but he couldn't find her. He thought of following her to Italy, but he knew she wouldn't come back, just as he knew he could never leave Skye.

'It's her,' sighed Roddy sadly. 'The same eyes, the same mouth . . . my Angelina.'

I didn't know what to say. It was kind of scary. It was just a dummy head, but for Roddy it was like she was a real person. And then there was that name, Florence. My mum's favourite city. The place we'd been going before it all happened. I sat down beside Roddy, my head bursting with memories. We sat for ages, watching the waves roll themselves in and drag themselves out, until the silence between us became unbearable and I decided to tell him about Mum.

How we were all ready to go on holiday and how Mum had gone to pick up the guide books from Auntie Dot's. How the driver behind her had seen it happen, seen her swerve to avoid hitting a stupid rabbit and instead she'd hit a tree. 2CVs are cool-looking cars, but they totally crumple on impact. She didn't stand a chance. The rabbit lived and Mum died.

I'd never talked about it before, not to anyone. Afterwards Roddy didn't say a word; he just put his arm round my shoulders. 'You should keep her,' I said, sniffing back tears and nodding at the head in Roddy's lap.

'I should,' he agreed.

'You should take her home.'

'No, I can't do that.'

'*Why?*'

'Because of Katie. She would not take kindly to me bringing Angelina back.'

'Then you should hide her somewhere safe.'

'I could keep her in my shed, but I'm too tired to walk back there now.'

'I'll take her. I have to go back that way, anyway.'

'That would be a kindness.'

64

'No problem.'

'And now I shall go home myself and tell Katie about the boat and the mannequins, but not about Angelina.'

'She'll be our secret,' I said.

'She will,' confirmed Roddy.

I took the head and walked back along the beach followed by Glen, who didn't seem to want to leave my side. I shouted after Roddy, but he was already out of sight and didn't hear me. When we reached the edge of the hazel wood Glen sat down on the rocks and wouldn't budge. There was no way he was coming inside. I left him there and walked across the mossy carpet to the little green hut. The door was still wide open and the empty whisky bottle lay where Roddy had left it on the floor. I picked it up and put it back on the shelf, then stood still and listened. The rustling of the leaves in the wind sounded like little voices sniggering. I placed the head in an old sack and left it under Roddy's chair. There was a small brass padlock with a key sitting on the worktop. I closed the door, then locked it, putting the key in my pocket.

'Stuff the fairies!'

8

Blue Flashing Lights

When I got back to the pink house I told Dad about Roddy's boat and finding the mannequins washed up on the beach, but I didn't tell him about Angelina. That was a secret between me and Roddy.

Dad said it had been on the radio. A small Greek cargo vessel called the *Athena* had almost gone down in the Black Skerries. It was on its way to America after dropping some stuff off at Greenock on the Clyde when it was caught in the storm. The captain radioed a Mayday, but the Air Sea Rescue couldn't get off the ground because of the wind and the lifeboat was already out rescuing the crew of a yacht that had sunk off Raasay. It looked like they were goners, but by some miracle the ship had cleared the Black Skerries and made the open sea, where it rode out the worst of the storm – but not before losing part of its cargo when a giant wave swept some crates off the deck.

'It must have happened just out there,' said Dad, pointing out of the kitchen window. 'It never ceases to amaze me how experienced sailors get themselves into these situations. They can't possibly have listened to the general synopsis, let alone the area forecast. It was all there in plain English – Storm Force Ten!'

'They were Greek,' I said.

'Even so.'

'Did they say anything about what was in the crates?'

'No, they didn't mention the contents. What about your friend Roddy? How's he going to manage without a boat?'

'I don't know. We thought that maybe if there was a reward for finding the mannequins he could maybe buy a new one. Have you any idea how much they cost?'

'Probably an arm and a leg,' laughed Dad.

The storm had played havoc with the rhubarb. It was lying in a tangled knot of broken pink stalks and wilting green leaves. Auntie Dot couldn't bear the waste so we spent most of Sunday making stewed rhubarb, gallons of it. Auntie Dot said it kept you regular, but how regular can you get?

Later on I started to worry about locking the

door of Roddy's shed. I knew it was Sunday and it was unlikely he'd be down on the beach, but what if he walked all the way to his hut to see Angelina and found it locked? I decided to return the key.

On the way there I kept to the high tide line and it wasn't until I reached the far end of the beach that I spotted the pile of assorted body bits we'd stacked neatly beneath the cliff. It looked totally unreal, like a scene from some gory movie. There were two large seagulls perched on the rocks and I noticed with a shudder that the blue paint of some of the eyes had been chipped away.

When I reached the croft there was no one home – even Glen was missing. I guessed they'd gone to church so I cut a short length of green nylon cord from an old fishing net, tied it round the key and hung it from the door handle. Roddy couldn't possibly miss it and as soon as he saw it he'd know what it was.

Monday it rained all day. Auntie Dot was the only one to venture outside. She came back wet and depressed because she'd killed a frog. Actually, she hadn't *really* killed the frog – at least not in a cold-blooded, premeditated, seriously bad karma kind of way. She just felt responsible for its death.

She'd found this frog sitting in the middle of the road waiting to be squashed by a huge black

Mercedes saloon car with tinted windows that was hurtling down the road as if it was in one of those car adverts. So she scooped it up and carried it to a small pond near the house, thinking she was doing it a big favour. The frog swam off to the other side and was promptly eaten by a heron, which had been standing dead still in the reeds watching it all happen. It obviously couldn't believe its luck. Meals on wheels, waitress service etc.

Auntie Dot was in tears when she told us. So were we, except ours were from laughing. At first I thought she was going to throw a wobbly, but eventually she saw the funny side too and laughed with us. There was no doubt about it: she was definitely getting better.

Tuesday was totally grey – it hardly seemed worth opening the curtains. Layers upon layers of lazy mist dragged themselves aimlessly over the island, loitering with the intent of making everything sopping wet. You could barely make out the edge of the field. It was Auntie Dot who spotted the blue flashing lights.

'What are they doing down there?' she asked.

Dad and I joined her at the kitchen window.

'Looks like the police, and maybe an ambulance,' said Dad solemnly, as if he were remembering too.

'Do you think there's been an accident?' asked Auntie Dot.

'I don't know,' said Dad. 'If it had been on the road you'd have thought we'd have heard it. They're parked right at the bottom of our field.'

'Perhaps we ought to go down and ask if we can help,' said Auntie Dot. 'It must be miles to the nearest hospital.'

Dad turned to me and I turned away. He put his hand on my shoulder.

'I'll go,' said Auntie Dot.

When she came back she was in a right state. She couldn't say anything, she just kept shaking her head and blowing her nose. Dad took her into the other room and closed the door. A while later he hobbled back in, looking as grey as the day outside.

'What's up?' I asked.

'It's your friend, the old man . . . He's dead.'

I couldn't say anything. I couldn't even cry. I couldn't believe this.

'It seems that he fell from the cliff top.'

'*How?*' I asked.

Dad shrugged his shoulders and sighed. 'I'm sorry,' he said.

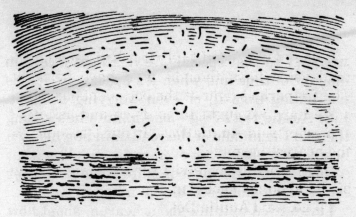

9

The Head of Angelina

For the first time in living memory Dad spent an
entire day without once mentioning the weather,
which must have been really difficult for him
because there was a major anticyclone over
Europe, forcing the depression over Scotland to
swing north over Scandinavia.

It was 'let's keep busy' time. We drove all
round the island, doing the proper tourist bit.
There were three days left and after Roddy's
death that seemed three too many. All I wanted
to do was get off this island and pretend none of
it had ever happened.

Dad and Auntie Dot never stopped talking. I
knew what they were up to. This was a
conspiracy of kindness, meant to distract me
from black thoughts. I tried thinking big brave
thoughts like, everyone's got to die otherwise life

wouldn't be that special. We've all got a certain amount of time and when it's up, it's up. It's no use hiding from it, or even worrying about it. Like Auntie Dot's frog – one minute he's sitting there in the middle of the road, minding his own business, probably not even understanding what a road is, and the next minute some do-gooder comes along and feeds him to a heron. Great!

I even tried to think about heaven, about how Mum and Roddy would already be there waiting for me. And how when I died I'd meet them and we'd all go fishing for mackerel, if God let you do that kind of thing. And I'd show Mum how to bait a hook and gut a fish. But then I started thinking maybe my time wasn't going to be up for ages yet and that I'd be an old man like Roddy and how was that going to work? Mum would still be young and might not even recognize me.

'Look at the light on the sea,' said Auntie Dot. 'Isn't it beautiful!'

I looked.

And I suppose it was.

On Thursday morning I was saved by Glen. Dad and Auntie Dot had another excursion planned and I didn't know how to tell them that there was only so much distraction I could take. Besides, the sun was shining and I wanted to be out in it, not watching it through a car window.

'Is that Roddy's dog?' asked Dad.

'Yes.'

'He seems to want something.'

'He probably wants a walk. I was thinking of walking over to the croft and seeing Katie. I haven't seen her since . . .'

'That's a lovely idea,' said Auntie Dot. 'You can take her these.' And she produced a huge tin of shortbread biscuits.

'Thanks.'

'Are you sure you'll be all right on your own for a bit?' asked Dad.

'Sure – besides I'll not be on my own, I've got Glen.'

The sun was shining and the sea was sparkling the same way it had been when we first arrived. The branches of the pines were swishing in the breeze and Glen was sniffing for rabbits amongst the foxgloves. Somewhere nearby I could hear the laborious groaning and clunking of heavy machinery. I looked up the hill and saw a yellow digger struggling with the rocky ground of the little churchyard and realized the hole it was trying to dig was probably for Roddy. I wondered whether that's what he'd have wanted, or whether he'd have preferred to be buried in the wood, or pushed out to sea in his boat, like the Vikings. And then I thought, It's not for him, it's for Katie, and besides, the *Angel of the Islands* wasn't going anywhere, not any more.

Katie was feeding the hens. She was dressed in black and even though she was always dressed in black this looked a blacker black than usual.

'Hello, Claude.'

'My Auntie Dot sent you these biscuits.'

'That's a kind thought. Would you like a cup of tea?'

I couldn't really say no. Katie disappeared into the kitchen and I sat down in front of the smouldering peat fire. There was a large grandfather clock standing in the corner of the room. I'd never noticed it before, but now its steady, remorseless tick seemed to fill the entire house. I watched as the minute hand shuffled towards the twelve, then listened as it began its solemn chimes.

'Ten o'clock,' said Katie, returning with a pot of tea. 'That's when the men came about those mannequins, ten o'clock on Monday morning. It seems so long ago.'

'Which men?' I asked.

'I think they said they were insurance investigators,' said Katie. 'They were both very nice. Italian, I think.'

'*Italian?*'

'That's what Roderick said.'

'How did they know the dummies were here?'

'Roddy told the minister on Sunday and the minister told the coast guard.'

'Did he show them the dummies?'

'Yes, they were very interested at first, but they said they were all too badly damaged to be worth anything. They had a good look round, but it seems they didn't find what they were looking for.'

'Did they say what that was?'

'No, but they did ask Roderick if there'd been any more mannequins washed ashore.'

'What did he say?'

'He said there might have been another head but he didn't know where it had gone. They gave him twenty pounds for his trouble and said if he found it there might be more money.' Katie reached over and took two ten-pound notes from the mantelpiece. 'Roderick insisted that one of these was for you.'

'No, honestly, I don't want it.'

'You should!'

'No, please keep it.'

Katie nodded and put it back on the mantelpiece; that's when I noticed the key to Roddy's shed still tied with the green nylon cord. He must have found it and put it there. The grandfather clock in the corner seemed to tick louder than usual. I thought about the head of Angelina lying in the sack in the shed. I couldn't work out why that particular head might be important to the insurance men, but I knew it was important to Roddy and I knew he'd want me to keep it safe, not just leave it there for the little dark people, or even the insurance people for that matter.

'I'm really sorry about Roddy,' I said.

'Yes,' sighed Katie. 'I don't know how it will be without him. There'll be no one to shout at, except Glen and the hens.'

'When did it happen?' I asked cautiously.

'Monday night. It was dark and the wind was blowing. Glen started barking and Roderick thought he heard voices. I told him he was being an old fool but he insisted on taking a look outside and then . . .' Katie started sobbing but pulled herself together. 'When he didn't come back I went outside myself and started shouting. I thought he'd gone for a walk to that shed of his. Him and his peppermints! Who did he think he was fooling? I took myself to bed and in the morning I walked to the telephone box and rang the police. They found him at the bottom of the cliff, lying beside those mannequins with Glen, here, at his side.' She blew her nose on her apron and Glen nudged her leg with his muzzle. 'You'll be wanting a cheese scone?'

'No thanks, I'd best get going.'

'Are you sure you won't take that ten pounds, Claude?'

'Positive – but could I borrow the key to Roddy's shed? There's something I left inside.'

'Of course you can.'

I walked down the path to the beach, staying high in order to avoid seeing the dummies. Glen followed close at my heels. He was quieter than usual. He must have seen it all happen . . . he knew. I picked up a stone and threw it, but he just watched as it clattered off the rocks. I knelt down beside him and stroked his back. He stared at me with his white eye, then turned towards the pine trees and began growling. The pines were a long way off but I could see what must have been spooking him – a speck of bright light glinting at the base of one of the trunks. Probably the sun reflecting off a piece of glass. 'Come on,' I said. 'It's not worth growling at. Let's get Angelina.'

Glen followed me reluctantly into the hazel wood. The green shed looked sad and lonely. I didn't waste any time. I unlocked the door and retrieved the head, still wrapped in the old sack. I was about to lock the door again when the fur on Glen's back suddenly rose. Slowly he lowered his head to the ground, letting out a long, low growl. 'What's up with you?' I asked, then heard the rustling of branches and the *crack* of a dead twig. Someone was coming! I didn't know who, but I knew I didn't want to meet anyone, not with the head of Angelina in the sack.

Leaving the door wide open, I grabbed Glen by the collar and dragged him round the back of the shed and into a thicket of ferns and foxgloves.

With my hands over his muzzle to stifle any growling I waited, peering through the curtain of leaves. I couldn't see anything but I could hear hushed voices. There were two of them. They were speaking in a different language. They must have been just on the other side of the shed. One of them muttered something like a curse, which was followed by clattering and crashing as all the tin cans and glass jars were swept off the shelves. Roddy's chair flew out of the door followed by tools and empty bottles. The place was being turned upside down. Eventually the door of the shed slammed shut and whoever it was began to talk more loudly. I still couldn't see them, but I could hear them clearly. They were the Italian insurance investigators. Glen shook his muzzle free and began to bark. I grabbed the sack and ran.

10

The Chase

I wasn't sure where I was going or why I was running. Glen was in the same kind of dilemma: he wasn't sure whether to defend Roddy's shed or follow me, but in the end he abandoned the shed and caught me up. The wood was wildly overgrown, a thick, tangled obstacle course of brambles and fallen trees with a few thousand nettles thrown in for extra discomfort. Glen took the lead, but had the advantage of being covered with fur. I could hear the other two behind us and by the sound of it they were having more problems than we were.

'*Stop!* We want to talk to you,' one of them shouted in English.

I thought about it briefly, but after I'd seen what they did to Roddy's shed I decided they'd have to catch me first.

It took ages to reach the path. Glen was already halfway up, barking for me to follow. My legs were covered with a red scribble of scratches from the brambles, burning through blotchy white nettle stings. I made a serious mental note never to wear shorts again. You just simply didn't know when you'd need the protection of a solid pair of jeans. Halfway up the path I stumbled and lost my grip on the sack. There was a sickening crunch and I knew instantly that the head was damaged, but there wasn't time to look. The insurance men had just broken cover. '*Stop!*' they shouted.

I kept running, trying to keep up with Glen, until I reached the road, where he was sitting wagging his tail. My first thought was to head for the house, but then I remembered that Dad and Auntie Dot were out and about. A large black Mercedes with tinted windows was parked in a lay-by further up the road. I didn't know what to do, but Glen did: he ran down the road, away from the car and away from the house. I slung the sack over my shoulder and ran after him.

One side of the road fell steeply into the sea and the other rose steeply up a barren hillside, completely devoid of cover. A few black-faced sheep took a break from nibbling the sparse grass and glanced unsympathetically in our direction. There was nowhere to hide. I was trapped on the road like a rabbit caught in a car's headlights. Glen kept stopping and barking, obviously frustrated that I couldn't keep up with him, but I was knackered. The sack was banging against my back and my legs felt like minced meat. All I wanted to do was to stop and sit down, until I heard the distant roar of a powerful car and the high-pitched squeal of its tyres as it leapt from the lay-by.

There was only one way to go and that was forward. About fifty metres further on there was a bend in the road and I knew that round that bend there was another lay-by, a much bigger lay-by, at a place called Lover's Leap where the drop from the road to the sea was spectacularly steep. There were nearly always a few cars parked there and usually a van selling teas, fizzy drinks and hot dogs. I could hear the car engine behind me getting louder, growling impatiently as it slowed for the bends. I kept running until I rounded the corner.

The van was there and beside it was parked a pale blue VW Beetle. Auntie Dot was walking cautiously towards it, trying hard not to spill two plastic cups of hot tea. Dad was propped up against our car with his binoculars trained on some stray wisps of cirrus uncinus that were brushing the distant mountaintops.

Auntie Dot looked up and dropped both cups. *'Claude!* What have you done to your legs?'

Dad dropped the binoculars. 'What's happened?'

The black Mercedes screeched round the corner, braked and skidded to a halt, peppering the side of the hot dog van with bits of flying gravel. Glen hurled himself at the driver's window, barking and clawing at the door.

'*What the blazes?*' exclaimed the hot dog man.

I ran to Dad and he put his arms round me. Glen backed off and positioned himself between us and the car with his body flat on the ground and his black lips curled into a menacing snarl. Both doors slowly opened and the two Italian insurance investigators stepped out.

The passenger wore a black suit and dark glasses. He was built like a bouncer, with concrete shoulders, no neck and a shiny shaved head. He stood in silence with one hand on the door frame and the other in his pocket.

The driver was much smaller and bonier with sharp angular features, definitely more of mackerel type than a haddock type. His hair was grey and cropped close to his skull. He wore narrow wire-framed glasses. His shoes were shiny, his trousers neatly pressed, his shirt immaculately white, and round his waist was strapped a dark blue bumbag.

'What's all this about?' demanded Dad.

Neither of them said anything. Bumbag knelt down and inspected the faint scratch marks that Glen had made on the driver's door. Glen growled. Bumbag stood back up and pointed to the sack, which was now at my feet.

'*That* is our property,' he said.

Dad looked down at me and then at the sack.

'It's not theirs. It's mine,' I said.

Dad bent down and peered into the sack. If he was surprised he managed to conceal it. 'Can you prove this belongs to you?' he asked.

'I do not need to,' replied Bumbag. 'It is part of the cargo that was washed ashore from the *Athena*.'

'Sounds like salvage then,' suggested the hot dog man, who had poured three cups of tea and seemed to be enjoying the confrontation.

'I am prepared to pay a reward,' said Bumbag.

'How much?' asked Dad.

'One hundred pounds,' said Bumbag.

Dad raised his eyebrows and looked at me. I shook my head.

'It is *our* property!' repeated Bumbag with obvious frustration.

'Two hundred,' suggested the hot dog man.

I shook my head again and stared at the ground.

'I will go to the police.'

'You do that!' said Auntie Dot. 'And while you're there tell them about your dangerous driving. There are laws in this country designed to protect innocent pedestrians – not to mention frogs.'

Bumbag now looked puzzled as well as flustered.

'And there's the damage to my van,' added the hot dog man, peering hopefully over the counter to see if he could see where the gravel had hit the rusting paintwork.

Bumbag muttered something Italian under his breath and got back in the car. Big Baldy followed him. The doors slammed shut and they drove off in another shower of gravel.

'Well! Really!' exclaimed Auntie Dot.

'Are you all right, Claude?' asked Dad.

'I'm OK.'

'What about your poor legs?' asked Auntie Dot.

'Sore.'

'Let's get you home,' said Dad.

'Free teas,' said the hot dog man.

I sat in the back with the sack on my lap and Glen at my feet. The car was full of questions that no one seemed to want to start asking. It was Dad who broke the silence.

'So what's so special about that head? What makes it worth a hundred pounds?'

'Maybe they thought I had something else,' I suggested and then explained about removing the dummy head before they'd ransacked Roddy's shed.

'I think we should report their behaviour to the police, don't you?' said Auntie Dot indignantly.

'Why do you want to keep it?' asked Dad, as if he hadn't heard her.

'Because it was special to Roddy,' I said.

Dad and Auntie Dot exchanged concerned looks, tacitly agreeing that the questions had gone far enough.

'Sentimental value,' suggested Auntie Dot sympathetically.

'Suppose so,' I mumbled.

'That's fine then,' said Dad.

The next day it was raining – not hard rain, but soft, misty rain. The kind that Scotland seems to specialize in. The anticyclone had moved north and east, settling over Norway and leaving in its wake an occluded front that Dad reckoned we'd be lumbered with for several days. We decided to go home. I left Dad and Auntie Dot packing and went to say goodbye to Katie.

'You'll be back,' she said.

Glen appeared in the doorway and dropped a wet pebble at my feet.

'Definitely,' I said.

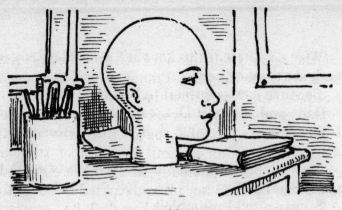

11

Inside the Head

The next few months were a confusing time. Dad and Auntie Dot had become an item. It wasn't exactly a big shock and I'd even grown to kind of like her, to like having her around. But sometimes her being there reminded me that Mum wasn't.

I knew it was serious because Dad had given up meat. He'd gone vegetarian on me and our kitchen cupboards had started to look like the shelves of some healthfood store. There were still sausages and bacon in the fridge but they were now stacked on the bottom shelf – *my* shelf – threatened on all sides by self-righteous looking pots of natural yoghurt and whiter-than-white lumps of Welsh goat's cheese. She hadn't exactly moved in, but they'd decided to be open and honest about it and had sat me down to tell me the news. I felt like I'd been smacked on the head with a cricket bat. I made myself a sausage sandwich and went upstairs.

The head of Angelina was sitting on my desk, staring forlornly into space. She was facing south-east in the general direction of Italy. I figured that's what Roddy would have expected her to do. I picked her up and carried her over to the window. The cracks on her skull had started oozing tiny balls of polystyrene foam like bits of brain.

I tried to prise one of the cracks open with the tip of my penknife. The jagged edge of fibreglass cut my fingertip and a drop of blood fell on the head. I tried again and this time a small section of head fell to the floor, followed by a shower of brain. Underneath I could see something shiny and black and when I poked it, it felt hard and lumpy. The head wasn't hollow – there was something else inside! I had to find out what.

I went downstairs, found a hammer and chisel in the garage and carefully began to open up the top of the skull. Beneath the polystyrene was a layer of thick black plastic and a label which said, FRATELLI CAMMISA – SCULTORI – FIRENZE. Feeling like some brain surgeon or bomb disposal expert, I tentatively removed the package and began opening it up. I don't know what I expected to find. I suppose I was half expecting gold, or jewels, or money, or even drugs. But not even in my wildest dreams did I expect to find *another head*.

It was small – about half life size – and carved out of wood. A beautiful woman with long hair that looked like it was blowing in the wind and an expression of shock or fear frozen on her face. I was completely stunned, not least because it was exactly the same expression of jokey, exaggerated surprise that Mum used to assume whenever Dad started on about the weather. It was like she was there, trying to make me laugh, but I didn't feel like laughing: the punchline was way below the belt and I crumbled into sobs, then tears – real anticyclone tears, the kind that leave puddles.

I heard someone rattling the garage door. It was Dad. I sniffed back the snot, wiped my face with the sleeve of my jumper, and hid the wooden head behind some old paint cans. I didn't want to show her to anyone, not even Dad. It was like having a dream that I wasn't ready to share. Later I moved her upstairs and hid her in the bottom of my rucksack, which was stuffed underneath my bed. Angelina went to live in the garden. We filled her with soil and planted deep purple pansies in the top of her head – they looked like curls of black hair.

It was a while before I started to think about Bumbag and began asking myself questions like, Had he known about the wooden head inside the dummy? Was that the real reason he'd ransacked Roddy's shed and then chased me halfway around Skye? Had Roddy really heard voices the night he fell off the cliff . . . and did he fall, or was he pushed? But the biggest question was, Who did I have stuffed in my rucksack under the bed? Someone had gone to a great deal of trouble to conceal her within the mannequin. I didn't have long to wait for the answer.

The Sunday papers fell with a thump on the floor and there she was in black and white on the front page. Beneath the photo was the caption 'Stolen Bernini' and the article:

INTERNATIONAL ART THIEVES SEND SHOCK WAVES THROUGH ITALY

The recent spate of art thefts from Italian museums has devastated the art world and continues to baffle the Italian police. The disappearance of Bernini's study of Daphne from the City Museum of Florence has confirmed suspicions that a well-organized ring of international art thieves is masterminding the theft and export of some of Italy's most valuable treasures. Signor Ricardo Balla, the director of the City Museum, says he is completely at a loss as to how the thieves were able to gain access to the museum and remove the priceless Bernini carving.

The theft took place on 22 May and seemed to be the culmination of a series of such thefts that over a period of six months have decimated some of the most important collections of Renaissance art in Italy. The City Museum has already had two similar incidents involving the disappearance of a Raphael portrait and a small bronze figurine by Michelangelo. There have been demands in the Italian press for the resignation of Signor Balla but his popularity and determination to step up security at the museum have thus far kept him his job. Signor Balla acknowledged that the theft of the Bernini carving was a particularly tragic loss as it is the only one of its kind in existence. Bernini was believed to have made the study in 1625 in preparation for what is considered his most famous sculpture, 'Daphne and Apollo', currently housed at the Villa Borghese in Rome.

There was more, but I'd read enough. It was slowly dawning on me what I had to do. I had to return the head to the museum in Florence – really I should have gone straight to the police and told them the whole story, but I couldn't go to the police, I couldn't even see a policeman in the street, or sitting in a car, without dreaming that awful dream. Taking the head to the police would have been like reliving the nightmare of Mum's death all over again. I had to change the ending and that meant doing it myself.

'Something interesting?' asked Dad, indicating the article he'd seen me reading.

'It's about Florence. About things being stolen from museums.'

Dad took the paper and stared at the photograph. I could tell he recognized that expression. 'It looks like . . .' he began, then stopped.

I nodded.

'Florence was your mum's favourite city.'

'I know.'

There was a long pause, then Dad asked, 'Would you like to go?'

I looked up at him, not believing I'd heard him say that.

'I can't go – I've had too much time off with that broken ankle – but Auntie Dot's thinking of going just after Christmas and she was wondering if you'd like to join her. She's staying with her friend, Professor Mason.'

'He was Mum's friend too,' I said defensively.

'He was their friend and their teacher,' he added. 'Your mum and Auntie Dot spent summers in Florence together.'

'I know.'

'Well then, what do you think?'

'I think I'd like to go.'

PART TWO

The Magic City

12

Nothing to Declare

Four days after Christmas Auntie Dot and I rose above the trough of low pressure that was smothering England in a grey blanket of freezing fog and soared into the clear blue sky on BA127 heading south-west over France, across the Alps towards Italy.

I love flying – I love everything about it, even hanging around airport departure lounges, checking in luggage and going through passport control. But this time there was a different edge to the excitement. Bernini's head of Daphne was wrapped up and stuffed inside my suitcase. I know I hadn't stolen it, but if anyone took it into their heads to look inside I'd have been up the creek without a paddle. What was worse, they'd probably assume it wasn't me but Auntie Dot who was the culprit and she didn't have a clue!

I had visions of her being interrogated by the Italian police, being force-fed salami until she cracked. Poor Auntie Dot – I almost felt guilty but I was reckoning on her unblemished karma getting us through at the other end.

I tried to put Bernini out of my mind, dream him away, but it was useless. I began flicking through one of the many volumes on Italian art that made up Auntie Dot's entire hand luggage allowance. Halfway through *Museums of Italy*, under the chapter entitled 'Rome', I found it – not just the head, but the whole body carved in white marble, being pursued by a lithe-looking Apollo. It was beautiful. A frozen moment in which so much was happening, it was almost impossible to think of it as solid and inert.

They were both running, with Apollo chasing Daphne. His arm was stretched out, his finger-tips touching her shoulder. Daphne could feel his touch, she knew the game was up. The face was the same as in the study but there were leaves in her hair and twigs and roots growing out from her fingertips and toes. It looked like she'd crashed into a tree.

'Wonderful, isn't it?' said Auntie Dot.

'Hmmm,' I muttered.

'It's a lovely story. Daphne was a beautiful wood nymph, a *virgin*,' she added, raising her eyebrows meaningfully. 'Apollo saw her and wanted her – typical man! But rather than be caught Daphne prayed to the gods to turn her into a laurel tree, which is exactly what they did. Look, you can see it happening at the very moment of their touching. Bernini was a genius.'

I closed the book, handed it back to Auntie Dot and looked out of the window. The edge of the plane's wing was glinting silver in the brilliant sunshine, a giant knife blade trembling over a jagged cake of snow-capped peaks. I watched as the peaks turned into a lumpy pastry crust of hills then fell away to a patchwork pancake of fields. The blade turned and began to descend towards a tangle of roads and terracotta rooftops.

'You didn't eat much,' said Auntie Dot as the stewardess whisked away an untouched ham sandwich.

'Not really hungry,' I replied.

'Better fasten our seat belts.'

It was late afternoon when we landed. I don't remember much about the airport. I was too nervous, too convinced there was an enormous label hanging round my neck saying, CLAUDE SCOTT – INTERNATIONAL ART SMUGGLER! but somehow we got through immigration control, collected our luggage and met Professor Mason. He was a short, stocky, older man wearing a denim shirt and jeans, standing to one side of the crowd, conspicuous by his snow-white hair and red face.

'There he is!' piped Auntie Dot, waving excitedly.

The professor smiled and casually raised a hand.

'Richard,' she said, kissing him politely on both cheeks, 'it's been simply ages.'

'Fifteen years,' said the professor, 'and you don't look a day older.'

'Oh, you can't possibly mean that,' said Auntie Dot bashfully.

'I most certainly do . . . as radiant as ever . . . a Botticelli Venus!'

'You're exactly the same as I remember you – silver haired and silver tongued.'

'Oh, I've been white haired and as wrinkled as a prune for as long as I can remember.'

'Are you still teaching?'

'By popular demand.' He turned his pale blue eyes on me and held out his right hand. 'Professor Mason at your service and you'll be Claude.'

I nodded.

'Pleased to meet you,' he continued. 'I imagine you'll be ready for a man-sized bowl of pasta.'

'Yes,' I said, suddenly feeling ravenous.

'Do you like clams?'

'I think so.'

'I have to, it's compulsory. I was born in Boston, where clams are the staple diet. My mother told me she spoon-fed me clam chowder

98

while I was still in diapers. Boston clams are out of this world but the Italians come up a close second with their baby clams. I bought a bagful this morning from the fish market so it's *spaghetti alle vongole* with fresh parsley and lots of garlic.'

'Sounds great.'

'See!' said the professor, looking at Auntie Dot and pointing at me. 'He's half Italian already.'

We all laughed and carried the bags to his car, an ancient Fiat 500 that didn't look capable of transporting a bag of clams let alone three people with luggage. It was parked directly outside the main door and was being scrutinized by a traffic policeman. I slowed down. Auntie Dot and I stood at a distance and watched as Professor Mason marched up to the policeman, who was busy making notes in a little book. It was fairly clear that he'd parked his wreck of a car somewhere he shouldn't have and I expected him to be full of apologies. It came as a bit of a surprise when he began arguing with the policeman. They were both flinging their arms about and shouting at each other in Italian. The policeman was pointing at the car and then pointing at the road. Professor Mason was pointing at his watch then pointing at the terminal building.

Auntie Dot was thinking beautiful thoughts and trying to stay calm. I was biting my lip, trying not to laugh. There was now a small crowd of people, mostly taxi drivers, gathering around the old Fiat listening to the argument. One or two of them had joined in. Everyone was shouting and pointing at different things. It was like watching one of those paintings in Auntie Dot's book come alive. I must have started laughing.

'I don't see what is remotely funny about this, Claude,' said Auntie Dot, who by now had turned the colour of a boiled shrimp. 'It's hardly a glowing example of civilized debate.'

The professor had opened the door of the Fiat and was throwing a pile of papers from the front seat into the back as if he was looking for something. He seemed to find it, then slammed the driver's door shut, at which point the door fell off its hinges and landed with a crash at the feet of the policeman.

This seemed to do the trick. For a second they all turned into statues and stared at the door and then they all began laughing, even the policeman and the professor. The professor opened his wallet and handed the policeman some money. The policeman picked up the dead door and presented it to the professor with all the mock solemnity of an Oscar ceremony. The professor played his part as well as any Oscar winner. He raised his eyebrows, shrugged his shoulders and took the door, clutching it to his chest. The taxi drivers applauded. Professor Mason took a bow and began to make a speech but then saw Auntie Dot and me and remembered why he was here. He leant the door against the car and walked over.

'Don't you just love it?'

Auntie Dot was temporarily lost for words.

'They just love a good argument. You can't do anything in Italy without a good argument. Let me take those bags.'

'What about the door?' asked Auntie Dot practically.

'The door?'

'The door that fell off.'

The professor shrugged his shoulders, tilted his head to one side and spread out his hands in a gesture of ambivalence.

'Perhaps we should get a taxi,' suggested Auntie Dot.

'Nonsense,' said the professor. 'Bessie would be mortally offended.'

'Bessie?'

'The car,' explained the professor patiently; 'your mode of transport, your limousine, your carriage, your wingèd chariot.'

Auntie Dot was unimpressed. It was going to take a seriously sustained sales pitch to convince her she wasn't about to dice with death.

'Bessie and I go back a long way,' added the professor fondly.

'That's perfectly apparent,' said Auntie Dot.

'Why Bessie?' I asked.

'Now there's an interesting question,' said the professor, brightening up. 'Bessie is named after my great-grandmother in America, who lived to the ripe old age of a hundred and two. She was still ploughing fields when she was ninety and was totally reliable,' he added, turning to Auntie Dot.

'If you say so,' she replied.

'I do. And now, your bags, madam. You sit in the front and you, young man, sit in the back behind me. Just throw those papers on the floor. It's going to be your job to hold the door in place on the way back home.'

When we were all inside the policeman and two of the taxi drivers relocated the wayward door while the others watched from mission control. The docking procedure was successfully completed with a roll of silvery grey adhesive tape, and with my hand firmly gripping the inside door handle Apollo 500 drove off towards Florence.

The professor was talking non-stop to Auntie Dot, presumably trying to take her mind off the various rattles and clanks emanating from the engine. He was what you might call an animated driver, constantly shifting position in his seat and turning round to talk. His hands seemed to barely touch the wheel. He was too busy pointing out the sights. Auntie Dot, by contrast, sat rigid, her wide eyes glued to the road with her hands gripping the edge of the seat. It wasn't so much a conversation, more a monologue to the doomed.

I gazed out of the window. We were in the middle lane of the main autostrada into Florence, hemmed in by enormous lorries on all sides. You could hear their engines roaring like hungry dinosaurs and their tyres hissing over the tarmac. Every now and then the lorries would thin out and between the gaps you could see roadside cafés festooned with fairy lights, set against a backdrop of inky black hills, which in turn were set against a backdrop of luminous colour. It was a cloudless night sky rising from brilliant blood red through orange and into pale green and then the deepest, most intense blue imaginable, speckled white with starlight. Ink-blot clouds of starlings, millions of them, were swimming like giant amoeba through the colours, flying to roost amongst the warmth of the ancient, sun-baked stones of Florence.

13

The Tower

That night I slept like a log – a deep, dreamless, timeless sleep that might have lasted well into the next day had it not been for the bells.

They began early in the morning just as it was getting light, invading the room and trespassing on my semi-consciousness like some insistent, half-forgotten dream from a different age. They were cavernous and solemn, almost apologetic, but like a dawn chorus of song birds they gathered momentum until only the deaf could possibly have slept. I lay still for a moment, gathering memories from the night before. Memories of narrow streets with tall, dark buildings and brightly lit shops, of a huge black door and an endless spiral staircase of stone steps worn smooth and rounded by centuries of tired feet. I was on the top floor of an ancient tower in the heart of Florence. I had a whole room to myself. It was better than any dream.

Pale pink early morning light streamed through enormous windows that ran the length of one wall. The other walls were covered with paintings, not just one or two, but dozens of them packed so close together they looked more like a gigantic stamp collection. I was lying on the sofa under a dark green duvet beside an old wood-burning stove and a pile of logs. On the table beside the sofa was a photograph of the professor – obviously taken some time ago – with an older lady. She looked familiar, but I couldn't think where I had seen her before. The floor was strewn with books, cushions and empty bottles of wine. The tabletops were covered in house plants, empty glasses and frozen rivers of candle wax that ran over the edge and into small, still pools on the floor. This place was seriously lived in.

I threw back the duvet and opened my suitcase, which was at the foot of the sofa. Bernini's head of Daphne was lying in the centre surrounded by bubble wrap in a nest of woollen jumpers. I lifted her out and began to peel away the wrapping. She seemed happy to be home. I gently placed her back in the suitcase face up, closed the lid, then walked over to the windows and stood there looking – looking at something I'd never seen, something I'd never imagined. It was as if I'd woken up in a lighthouse surrounded by a sea of orangey brown tiled roofs. They seemed to stretch for miles and miles to a distant shore of tiny black trees and pale blue mountains. Other towers rose from amongst the waves like the masts of ships, and huge, domed buildings stood proud like desert islands promising hoards of buried treasure. I pulled back the handle and opened the window. Cold fresh air swam into the room carrying with it the clear crisp resonance of the last bell.

'You're up early!'

I turned round and saw Professor Mason.

'The bells,' I said.

'Ah! *The bells, the bells*,' he echoed, doing a pretty good Quasimodo impersonation. 'You'll get used to them . . . after twenty years or so. Did you sleep well?'

'Like a log.'

'Do you fancy some breakfast?'

'Please.'

'Let's go out. The kitchen smells like the Boston fish market.'

'Is Auntie Dot up yet?'

'Dorothy's already communing with culture. She left half an hour ago armed with her guide books. She sends her apologies and says she'll make it up to you by spending the rest of your holiday as your tour guide. I don't imagine there'll be a single museum in Florence that won't have come under her scrutiny by the end of her stay. She always was diligent beyond belief.'

'You were her art history professor?'

'Many moons ago – a summer school at the university. But let's quit this "professor" malarkey: call me Ricardo – everyone else does.'

'You taught my mum too.'

'Yes,' he said more seriously. 'Daisy and Dorothy, chalk and cheese. I was so sorry to hear about . . .' His voice trailed off and he looked away across the rooftops up into the brightening sky where the amoeba swarms of starlings were now flying away from the city, out towards the distant farmland with its rich pickings of insects and grubs.

'Breakfast!' he repeated. 'And afterwards we'll drive to the station and meet my daughter.'

He paused for effect and raised his eyebrows mischievously. 'Claude and Claudia – that's her name, although in Italy you pronounce it "Cloudia".'

I felt a slight stab of annoyance at the thought that he was trying to pair us off, but I figured she must be at least Auntie Dot's age and might be good company for her and get me off the hook. After all, I had my own plans which, although they involved museums, were very different from Auntie Dot's.

We had breakfast in a little café on the corner

of the piazza just opposite the tower. It was cold when we first stepped outside, a sharp dry cold, and the warmth of the café was a welcome diversion. The professor had a cappuccino, I had freshly squeezed orange juice and we both demolished two enormous sticky pastries. The café was busy; everyone seemed to know everyone else. This was the early morning rush hour, Italian style.

When we left, the sun was that bit higher in the sky and the piazza was already a few degrees warmer. We walked over to Bessie, who was parked in the shadows beneath the tower. Someone had drawn a heart with an arrow through it in the dirt on her bonnet.

'Don't you just love it?' exclaimed the professor. 'God bless Italians, they appreciate beauty when they see it!'

14

Oranges and Sausages

The main railway station was on the other side of the city and the main road to it, which ran alongside the river, was very busy. The professor took a short cut, weaving down dark, narrow alleys barely wide enough to accommodate a Fiat 500 and a skinny pedestrian, but somehow he managed it. We arrived as the express train from Rome was disgorging its passengers onto Platform 21.

We stood at the end, surrounded by a flock of scraggy-looking pigeons fighting over a discarded pizza crust. The birds scattered as the throng of passengers approached. It was like some mad fashion parade – everyone jostling for space on the catwalk, showing off their winter collection of woollens and furs. Most of them were carrying large bags bulging with colourfully wrapped parcels. Probably late Christmas presents brought from Rome.

I had no idea who we were looking for but there seemed to be at least six likely candidates, all about Auntie Dot's age and dressed to the nines. They all walked past and the professor didn't even blink. He was still staring down the platform towards the tail end of the fashion parade where there were two more possibilities, neither of which looked a likely culture vulture and suitable companion for Auntie Dot. My heart sank.

'Claudia!' shouted the professor.

Neither of the women acknowledged him, but a young girl with longish brown hair and a rucksack slung over her shoulder stopped and waved. The professor walked over and gave her a hug.

'Hi, Dad.'

'I hardly recognized you,' said the professor. 'You must be a good six inches taller.'

'Two,' said the girl.

'Two . . . six, what's the difference?'

'Four?'

The professor smiled and she smiled back.

'How's Mom?'

'She's fine,' said the girl, looking across at me.

'Claudia, this is Claude. Claude, this is Claudia,' said the professor, obviously enjoying himself.

'Hello,' I said.

'Hi,' replied Claudia.

We stood looking at each other. She was about my age with a longish face and dark brown eyes that never seemed to blink. She was dressed like a boy in a blue ski jacket, faded jeans and scruffy trainers. She looked kind of tough, but also kind of shy.

'Have you brought Bessie?' she asked the professor.

'We have, but I thought you two might walk back together.'

We both looked at him and then at each other.

'Why?' asked Claudia.

'I've got to drive on to the university and sort out a few things.'

'Can't we go with you?'

'It's just administration – answering e-mails, admissions, boring stuff like that. Besides, young lady—'

'Don't!' interrupted Claudia. 'You know I hate it when you call me that.'

'Besides,' continued the professor, 'you've been sitting on a train for hours and I'm sure the last thing you need, or want, is to be sitting in a car and then in a stuffy old office. Stretch your legs, get to know each other, show Claude Florence. He's only just arrived.'

Claudia lowered her eyebrows and frowned at her father. I felt like I should be somewhere else,

111

anywhere else – even ticking off pages in the guide book with Auntie Dot. Then Claudia turned to me, raised her eyebrows and almost smiled.

'Come on then,' she said, letting her rucksack drop from her shoulder and handing it to the professor. 'We'll see you back at the tower.'

She turned and started walking out of the station with her hands shoved deep down into the pockets of her ski jacket. I turned to the professor, half expecting him to say something, but he just winked. I ran after Claudia.

'Claudia!' shouted the professor.

She didn't answer.

'Have you got your key?'

'Yes,' she replied without turning round.

I was walking fast but it was still a job keeping up with her. I stayed a couple of paces behind, following her down the steps to the main road. She took them three at a time and it was only when she got to the bottom that she turned round to see if I was still there. Even then she didn't say anything. She turned her attention to the tangle of traffic that was slowly but steadily circumnavigating the massive station building. She saw a gap and ran out into the thick of it, weaving in and out of the lanes, skipping between cars, lorries and motor scooters like some forest nymph dancing through the trees – except these trees were moving at speed.

When she reached the other side she didn't look round but kept on walking. I was going to lose her. I took a quick look. There weren't any lights or proper pedestrian crossings so I didn't have much choice. I waited for a similar small gap in the moving traffic and stepped out, only to have a motor scooter miss me by inches and an open-backed van stacked high with crates of oranges slam its brakes on in front of me. Four of the topmost crates crashed onto the road and hundreds of oranges rolled out into the traffic, waiting to be squashed to pulp.

Cars started honking their horns. People were rolling down their windows, some of them laughing, others shouting. The driver of the van jumped out. He was tearing at his hair and spitting words in my direction that I guess you wouldn't have found in the average phrase book. It was no use trying to apologize. I couldn't speak Italian and perhaps it was just as well. A quick exit was called for. I thought briefly about returning to the station steps, but decided I'd be safer risking the crossing.

The traffic had slowed down and everyone seemed to be having fun seeing how many oranges they could squash. The poor van driver was going ballistic. I just kept walking slowly, figuring that was my best chance, all the time imagining myself being lifted back onto a plane with two broken legs and Bernini's head of

Daphne still safely hidden inside my suitcase.

No one stopped but they all managed to avoid me and eventually I reached the other side with nothing worse than a pair of sticky trainers from where I'd waded through the river of orange juice. Claudia was doubled up with laughter.

'That was the funniest thing I've seen for ages,' she said between gasps for air.

'*Funny!*' I said with real anger. 'You call that funny?'

'All those oranges!' she laughed. 'That poor guy's face!'

'I was nearly killed,' I said in exasperation.

'Look! He's still trying to pick them up,' she screamed.

I looked back as the van driver stood up cradling an armful of oranges. He saw me, gritted his teeth and took a step towards us only to have to jump back again as a taxi cab swerved to miss him. The oranges he'd rescued dropped to the ground. The taxi driver stopped the cab, climbed out and started yelling at him. He started yelling back. It wasn't his day.

'Let's get out of here,' said Claudia.

We ran through the streets like escaped convicts and didn't stop until the clamour of the station was far behind us. It was Claudia who decided when to stop. She was ahead of me, making the decisions, ducking and diving from one street into another, taking me on a whirlwind tour of Florence. She staggered to a halt halfway down one of the quieter streets where four piglets sat at a tiny table eating sausages. They were real piglets that had been stuffed. It was sick. They were holding knives and forks and had red and white checked napkins tied round their necks and little Father Christmas hats on their heads. It was cannibal party time.

Claudia was standing with her forehead pressed against the glass of the shop window, panting. I stopped alongside her and did the same. The cold of the glass felt good. I didn't say anything. I was too out of breath. I just looked in total amazement at carnivore heaven. This place was wall to wall meat – pig meat dried and cured in every conceivable shape and form: legs, heads, trotters, ears, salami, pepperoni, hams. Endless strings of dark red sausages hung from the ceiling like stalactites of blood – a massive beaded curtain of pig. It was a vegetarian's image of the gates of hell.

'I know what you're thinking,' said Claudia, still with her forehead pressed against the glass but moving her eyes so that we were looking at each other's reflection against the backdrop of dried meat.

I turned and looked at her, not sure what to say.

'I'm psychic,' she said.

115

'Go on then,' I challenged.

'You think I'm a brat.'

'No I don't,' I insisted, knowing I'd been thinking exactly that all the time we'd been running.

'You're also thinking that Ricardo's old enough to be my grandad.'

She was right. I *had* been thinking that, but that didn't make her psychic. They were both reasonable guesses.

'What am I thinking now?' I asked.

'You're wondering whether I'm really psychic.'

Another reasonable guess.

'You don't believe me, do you?' she said, standing up straight and shoving her hands back into the pockets of her ski jacket.

'You tell me – you're the psychic one,' I said.

She smiled. 'My Italian grandmother was psychic – that's my mother's mother. It tends to skip a generation. My mom's not psychic at all; neither's my dad.'

'How old's your mum?' I asked, starting to feel more at ease.

'Thirty-six.'

'How old's your dad?'

'Sixty-four. That's a difference of twenty-eight years. So yes, he's old enough to be my grandad.'

'Are they . . . ?'

'Not any more. They split up eight years ago. My mom lives in Rome. She and Dad are divorced and she's now married to this Australian

116

sculptor called Bruce. He welds wrecked cars together, sprays them wild colours and sells them for a fortune.'

I just nodded. What could you say? I was beginning to wonder if there was any point in saying anything at all. She seemed to know the questions as well as the answers. Maybe she really was psychic.

'I think I know why you're here,' she said seriously.

'Why?' I asked, thinking this time I'd got her.

'You're looking for something. I know what it is. It's your mum. That's not being psychic, that's because Dad told me about her, but I also know you're here to bring something back. I don't know what. I just feel it.'

This took me completely by surprise.

'I can help if you like,' she said.

'With what?' I asked, not wanting to give anything away.

'With finding your mum. I've heard a lot about her from my dad and I feel I know her favourite places in Florence. I can show you them.'

Suddenly I felt really uneasy again. It was as if this girl had gatecrashed my head. She was there inside, flipping through my most private thoughts and feelings like someone browsing in a bookshop.

'If you want to go . . .' she added.

I looked down at the piglets and thought about

what she'd said. Apart from bringing back the Bernini the big attraction of Florence was knowing that Mum had been here, that it was her favourite city. I wanted to see the same things she'd seen, feel the same feelings. I imagined it would just happen; that if she loved something I would love it too, but I'd always thought of it as one big single experience. Obviously she'd have had favourite places, places that were more special and meaningful than others. And these were the places where I'd be closest to her. But, as much as I wanted to, did I really believe in Claudia's psychic powers?

'This was one,' she said, nodding towards the window we'd just been staring into. 'That's why I stopped here.'

I glanced back at the beaded curtains of pig, remembering how Mum had loved sausages. Claudia was looking at me with those dark brown unblinking eyes. I knew she was telling the truth. I knew I could trust her. She took me on the 'Daisy Scott Tour of Florence'. It wasn't what I expected. There were a couple of obvious tourist magnets like the cathedral and the bridge with the shops. But mostly I found myself outside cafés that served the very best cappuccinos and shops that sold beautiful marbled wrapping paper. It was like playing hide and seek with a ghost. I found myself discovering a mum I'd never really known. A young mum who was here before I was born. And I loved it.

The last stop on the tour was the Uffizi Gallery. We paid our entrance fees and Claudia dragged me through until we were standing in front of the most beautiful painting I'd ever seen in my life. It was by an artist called Simone Martini, who was famous hundreds of years ago and I guess is even more famous now. His painting was called *The Annunciation*. Mum had shown me a picture of it in one of her books but nothing could have prepared me for the shock of the real thing. It was huge and mostly gold. It was of a gentle angel kneeling on the ground talking to a frightened Virgin Mary. Words were flowing from the angel's mouth. Time seemed to stand still and I was there in the picture listening to that same angel.

'This was your mum's favourite painting,' whispered Claudia.

'I know,' I said. 'She showed me pictures of it in books.'

'She told Dad it was so beautiful that she could only look at it for thirty seconds. Any longer and she'd be lost. It would do her head in.'

I nodded, understanding how she'd felt.

'They've got a ward in the hospital in Florence for people who've done their heads in looking at art. It's called the Art Lag ward.'

I took one last look at the lips of the angel and believed every word.

15

The Priceless Panettone

The next morning at breakfast Auntie Dot was full of it. She was talking non-stop, stringing together artists and dates the way Dad strung together frontal systems and wind speeds. She'd *done* the Uffizi and half of Florence. She'd absorbed so much culture it was leaking out of her and she seemed unaware that no one else was really listening, just as she seemed unaware of the bowl of pale green grapes on the table that had been plucked from the vine earlier that morning and were glistening with dew.

'Eat!' commanded the professor, nudging the bowl towards her.

Auntie Dot looked at the grapes with mild curiosity, lifted one from the top and popped it in her mouth.

'You can have another,' said the professor, winking mischievously.

'Oh I know, I'm being a pain. Just tell me to shut up,' said Auntie Dot, smiling self-consciously. 'I'm just so excited to be back. There's so much to see. I thought we'd do the cathedral collection this morning and perhaps try and squeeze in the Michelangelos and Giottos before lunch.'

Claudia and I exchanged glances of dismay.

'You do realize,' began the professor, 'that if you step outside into the piazza you'll see a man with as many noses on his face as there are days left in the year.'

'*Dad!*' said Claudia, raising her eyebrows in mock disdain. 'You *always* say that.'

'Pardon?' asked Dot. 'I'm afraid I don't understand.'

'New Year's Eve,' explained Claudia patiently. 'One day – one nose.'

It took a couple of seconds to sink in.

'Silly me,' sighed Dot. 'I completely forgot.'

'And most of the museums will be closed,' added the professor.

Auntie Dot looked crestfallen.

'Except . . .'

Her eyes widened.

'The City Museum. It will be open this afternoon between one and four-thirty.'

She breathed a huge sigh of relief. She was obviously seriously addicted.

'However,' continued the professor, 'there's the small matter of a party to organize. That means food, wine, fireworks, and I shall need some fetchers and carriers.'

'Of course,' said Dot, putting on a brave face.

'No, not you, Dot,' laughed the professor. 'The fountains and frescos of Florence await your perusal. Claudia and Claude will suffice.'

Auntie Dot descended the well-worn stone steps of the tower armed with her guide books and a few minutes later the professor, Claudia and I followed suit. The sky was grey and the air was cold and damp. We pulled up the collars of our coats and dug our hands deep into the pockets. A layer of mist like some ghostly snake lay sleeping on the river. It felt like the end of a long year, as if everything had wound down and was only just ticking over with the aid of the essential life-supporting smells of fresh coffee and pizza. The fetching and carrying was over by mid-morning. The professor made some excuse about a lunch appointment and left Claudia and me together in the tower.

'What should we do?' I asked.

'You should do what you came to do,' she replied.

'What do you mean?'

Claudia said nothing – just stared at me with those eyes. It was spooky.

'You know, don't you?' I said.

'I know you've got to do something when you're here. Something important.'

It was no use pretending. It was like my skull was made of glass and she could see everything inside.

'I found something in Scotland last summer. Something valuable that belongs here in Florence.'

'You don't need to tell me if you don't want to,' she said seriously.

'I want to,' I said. 'I need your help.'

So I told Claudia about Skye – about Roddy and Katie, about Bumbag and the dummies on the beach, about the head of Angelina and the head inside the head. When I lifted it from my suitcase and carefully removed the bubble wrap Claudia gasped and put her hand over her mouth.

'I know,' I said, feeling secretly pleased that I'd actually managed to surprise her.

'Do you . . . ?' she began.

'What?'

'Do you know what that is?'

'It's Bernini's study for the head of Daphne, carved sometime in the early sixteen hundreds and recently stolen from the City Museum here in Florence.'

The brown eyes blinked. 'What are you going to do?'

'I'm going to hand it in.'

'To the police?'

'No, the museum. I can't go to the police.'

'Why not?'

'I just can't.'

'But—'

'I just can't, OK? Not since . . .'

'OK. You don't need to tell me,' she said understandingly.

'I should do it today,' I said. 'The last day of the old year. But you don't have to come with me. I just need you to show me where the museum is.'

'I'd like to come,' she said.

'It shouldn't be dangerous,' I said, feeling kind of relieved. 'Nobody need know we've got it. I thought I'd just leave it somewhere and let someone find it.'

'You can't do that!'

'Why?'

'You don't know who might find it, or what they might do with it.'

'Suppose so.'

'If you're going to leave it anonymously you should leave it somewhere like outside the director's office. At least that way you're fairly sure that whoever finds it will be a responsible member of staff.'

I nodded in agreement.

'When do you want to do it?'

'Sooner the better,' I said, 'except . . .'

'Except what?'

'It's the only museum open and Auntie Dot will be there as soon as the doors open at one. I don't want her to see us.'

'Let's leave it till later then. Dad says it closes at four-thirty so if we go inside at about four that'll give us half an hour. Have you thought about what you're going to carry it in?'

'Plastic bag?' I said, shrugging my shoulders.

'No!' said Claudia emphatically. 'I'm sorry but you can't carry something like this round the streets of Florence like it was a salami.'

'What do you suggest then?'

'I don't know, but it should be something that has a bit more dignity about it. Something that's not too conspicuous . . . I know!'

'What?'

'A panettone box.'

'A *what*?'

'Panettone – the cake. It's a special Italian thing. Everyone buys one for Christmas and New Year. They give them as presents. The streets will be full of people carrying panettone boxes and they're the perfect shape. Remember, Dad bought two this morning. They'll be with the rest of the shopping downstairs.'

We carried Daphne down to the kitchen, where two pale blue panettone boxes sat on the table. Claudia opened one, removed the head-sized cake and placed it on a plate. Then with due care we lined the inside with cotton wool from the bathroom and lowered the precious carving inside. It was a perfect fit and when the box was closed there was even a little plastic handle with which to carry it.

At four o'clock we were standing in a small queue of people waiting to buy tickets. The walk across town had been straightforward. Claudia knew Florence like the back of her hand and the streets, as she predicted, were full of panettone-carrying pedestrians. I was just one of the crowd but now that we were actually inside the hushed and hallowed atmosphere of the museum the panettone box I was carrying seemed to be glow-ing with guilt.

Claudia paid for the tickets then walked towards the entrance to the collection. A uniformed guard took our tickets and scrutinized them one at a time. This was worse than passport control. His eyes wandered from the tickets to our faces and then down to the box. He said something to me in Italian and, trying to look as innocent as possible, I shook my head and turned to Claudia, who began talking. The guard pointed at the box and I felt my legs turn to jelly. Claudia said something else then he started laughing and ushered us both inside.

'What was that all about?' I whispered.

'He wanted us to leave the box with him.'

'*What?*' I exclaimed. 'What did you say?'

'I said no fear. I said he had suspicious eyes and he'd probably eat it before we got back.'

The box bumped against my leg and I could hear the head of Daphne tapping against the cardboard. We walked from room to room, pausing at each doorway to check for the telltale mop of steely grey hair, but Auntie Dot must have been here, and done here, before we arrived.

The offices were on the top floor at the very back of the building but it was important to take our time, to play the part of museum visitors and not draw unwanted attention to ourselves. We lingered with the crowds in front of serene Madonnas with the kind of skin that sells soap and the kind of smile that sells anything. I know it sounds ridiculous, but all those smiling faces made me feel as if they approved. I was bringing them back Daphne and everything was going to work out.

At 4.20 we were standing at the top of a huge stone staircase, looking into the last room of the museum. It was darker than the rooms downstairs and mostly empty except for two security guards at the end. Perhaps they'd turned off the lights as it was nearly closing time. The paintings on the walls looked almost black. There were no smiling faces here.

127

'The offices are over there,' whispered Claudia, nodding to her right where across the polished marble floor you could see a row of imposing-looking doors. The one at the end glittered with gold leaf and was larger and more imposing than the others. 'That'll be the director's office,' she said.

I looked down at the blue panettone box and then glanced at the two security guards.

'Go on!' urged Claudia.

I walked across the floor towards a life-sized sculpture of a sleeping child lying stretched out on a granite base. The sculpture was in smooth white marble, the eyelids heavy and closed, the tiny fingers folded neatly across the chest. This wasn't sleep – this was death. There was a clatter of footsteps behind me and I turned to see a small woman dressed in black, holding a sheet of white paper in her left hand. She walked right past me towards the imposing golden door and was just about to knock on it when it opened and out stepped Bumbag!

'Signor Balla!' she said reverentially, before they both disappeared inside. I stood frozen to the spot, as still as the child on the marble tomb.

'Psssst,' whispered Claudia. 'Leave it!'

'I can't.'

'The guards,' she mouthed silently, holding a hand to her face as if yelling and at the same time nodding down the dark room to where the two security guards were marching towards the stairs.

'I can't leave it – I'll explain later,' I said as the footsteps echoed behind us.

Claudia screwed up her face, clearly exasperated.

'*Il museo è chiuso*,' said the nearest guard.

16

Fratelli Cammisa

'So tell me again, but slowly,' said Claudia.

It was already dark outside and had started to rain. We were sitting at a table in a small café opposite the museum sipping hot chocolate.

'It was Bumbag! Signor Balla, the museum director, is the same person who was posing as an insurance investigator on Skye.'

'Are you sure?'

'*Positive!*'

'Then that means . . .'

'Exactly. *He* must have stolen the head in the first place. That's what he was looking for on Skye. He must have been trying to smuggle it to America hidden inside the dummy head when the storm washed it overboard.'

'He must have been seriously razzed off!'

'He was.'

'Do you think he knows you still have it?'

'He can't know for sure because he never actually saw what was in the sack.'

'But he suspects.'

'Probably.'

'Then he'll be a worried man, worried about you finding what was inside and putting two and two together.'

'I know. And I was going to make him a New Year's Eve present of it!'

I looked at the panettone box, which was on the floor beside me. A family came in and sat down at the table next to us carrying two identical panettone boxes. Behind the counter of the café was a shelf lined with about twenty others. They were everywhere.

'This gets crazier by the minute,' said Claudia. 'So what now? I know you don't want to go to the police, but there doesn't seem any alternative.'

'Do you think they'd believe us?' I asked.

Claudia stared into her hot chocolate. 'Probably not. At least not without some proof. But you could give them the head. Maybe even leave it outside with a note.'

I took a sip of hot chocolate and shook my head.

'Not a good idea,' she agreed.

'Apart from anything else,' I said, 'if we give the head to the police they'll just give it back to Bumbag, and who knows what he'll do with it?

It'll probably be in the news again in a couple of days when he claims that thieves have broken into his impregnable museum and nicked it for a second time.'

We finished the hot chocolate and sat watching the rain drip from the awning outside the café onto the glistening pavement. Across the street the steps of the museum were deserted and only four lights remained on inside – three upstairs and one downstairs. One by one the upstairs lights went out. A few minutes later the front door opened and two people stepped out into the rain. It was Bumbag and the short lady dressed in black. They stood talking for a while as they put up their umbrellas. Then they hurried down the steps in opposite directions.

'That's him!' I said.

'Bumbag?' Claudia asked.

'Yes.'

'Let's follow him,' she suggested.

I didn't think twice; I reached down, grabbed the panettone box and we ran out of the café.

Bumbag was on the opposite side of the street, head bent, with his black umbrella leaning into the rain. Following him was a piece of cake. The rain was a perfect cover. He walked quickly and deliberately like someone who knew where he was going and was in a hurry to get there. He stopped only once outside an expensive shoe shop but I don't think he was interested in the

132

shoes. I think he was checking that he wasn't being followed. Claudia and I were on the opposite side of the road outside a restaurant. We both pretended to be looking at the menu. Bumbag looked around him and seemed satisfied that he was on his own. He set off again, this time down a narrow, dark alley leading towards the river.

This was more difficult. It was still raining but the alley was empty and the sound of our footsteps echoed off the dark walls. If he turned round now he'd spot us for sure so we hung back, hiding behind a parked van in order to let him get ahead. In the distance we heard the creak of a door opening and then a slam as it shut. We ran down the alley until we reached the river.

'We've lost him,' panted Claudia.

'Damn!' I said.

'He's got to be there somewhere,' she insisted, staring back up the alley.

'Let's take another look,' I suggested.

By now we were both soaked. We wandered back, weaving from one side of the alley to the other checking all the doors. About halfway up I spotted the sign: FRATELLI CAMMISA – SCULTORI.

'This is it!'

'How do you know?'

'There was a label on the plastic when I first opened the dummy head. That's what it said – Fratelli Cammisa.'

133

'Cammisa brothers – sculptors,' said Claudia, looking up at the sign.

We stepped back out into the alley and looked up at the building. It was really tall, about five storeys high, and there was a faint glow coming from the top-floor windows.

'So what now?' asked Claudia, her brown hair hanging in wet rats' tails round her shoulders.

'I suppose we should get back,' I said half heartedly.

'They'll be expecting us,' she agreed, but with the same lack of conviction.

We were both staring at the door handle.

'Try it!' urged Claudia. 'It's not locked.'

'How do you know?'

'Try it.'

I turned the handle and the door swung open, revealing a dark, dingy hallway and a set of stairs.

'What do you think?' whispered Claudia.

'You tell me,' I whispered back.

She edged past me and crept up the first flight of stairs like a cat. I closed the door behind me quietly and followed her trail of wet footprints. She was waiting on the first-floor landing. All the doors were closed and the whole place was as quiet as a tomb. She didn't say anything – just raised her eyebrows and nodded upwards. We kept climbing until we reached the top, where a folded black umbrella stood point down in a small puddle of rainwater outside a half-opened door. We stood still as statues listening for signs of life but there was nothing, not even the creak of a floorboard. I handed Claudia the panettone box and, holding my breath, stuck my head round the door.

I nearly died on the spot. The entire room was packed with naked people all standing perfectly still. I wanted to shut the door and run but I couldn't move. I was petrified. And then I realized that what I was looking at wasn't real people at all.

'*What is it?*' whispered Claudia urgently.

'It's full of dummies,' I whispered back. 'Hundreds of them.'

'Let's see.'

She opened the door a little wider and gazed in wide-eyed amazement at the petrified party. All the mannequins were life sized, pink and faceless, frozen in bizarre poses as if they'd all suddenly stopped dancing. None of them had painted eyes or lips, but you could feel them looking at you – looking and listening.

'This must be the warehouse where they store them,' I said.

'Spooky,' whispered Claudia.

'Seriously,' I whispered back, remembering the day on Skye when I'd found the dummies washed up on the beach.

Beyond them at the far end of the long room a

single fluorescent strip light flickered on the ceiling above a table and six empty chairs. On the table was something large and pink.

'I think we should get out of here,' whispered Claudia.

'Just a second,' I whispered back. 'I want to see what that is on the table.'

'It's a leg,' she said. 'Probably a dummy's leg, but I'm not sure I want to find out.'

Behind the table were windows looking out onto the alley and on either side freshly painted limbs hung from the walls. One wall, legs, the other, arms. Beneath the windows was an attentive audience of torsos complete with heads. But there was definitely something odd about the lone leg lying in the centre of the table like exhibit 'A'. It crossed my mind that it was probably already packed with some stolen masterpiece ready for shipping. That's all we needed to go to the police. That's why Bumbag was here.

'Let's go,' I whispered. But as the words left my mouth a door at the far end of the room swung open and four men walked in. We froze amongst the dummies, barely breathing, willing ourselves to become naked, pink and faceless. There was a scraping of chairs as the four men took their places around the table. Apparently they hadn't noticed us.

One of the men was Bumbag. He was sitting

with his back to us. The other three sat opposite, facing us and the dummies, but their eyes were all on Bumbag. I wanted to turn round and look at Claudia but I didn't dare move. Even the blinking of my eyelids seemed like a dead giveaway.

The man in the middle was much older than the others and seemed to be in charge. He had a huge bald head speckled like granite with brown age spots, sagging jowls and heavy drooping eyelids that half hid his hard, black eyes – the kind of eyes that looked like they'd seen too much already. He was wearing a black suit and must have weighed well over a hundred kilos. He sat with his podgy hands resting on the table, glaring directly at Bumbag over the top of the dummy leg. The two other men sat on either side of him. They were younger but equally huge. They might have been his sons. One of them looked like Big Baldy, Bumbag's henchman on Skye.

Bumbag was talking. You could tell he was nervous. Next to these three he looked like a scrawny sparrow cornered by three carnivorous crows. Granite Head slowly raised one of his podgy hands. It glittered with heavy gold rings. Bumbag stopped talking and began listening. Granite Head's voice was a deep, laborious rumble like some distant rock fall in a mountain pass. Bumbag seemed to be answering questions but not making a very good job of it.

We were about twenty metres from the table and surrounded by dummies. The door to the stairway was only ten metres to our right. Whatever was going on at the far end of the room was obviously absorbing all their attention. If we were going to sneak out it had to be now. I turned slowly to find Claudia amongst the dummies. She was standing behind the pink faceless figure of a woman with outstretched arms and behind her was the black figure of a man with outstretched arms, except this figure had a face.

The arms clamped round Claudia's chest. She screamed and I leapt to help her as another black figure stepped through the door and closed it behind him. The man who held Claudia pushed me aside and I fell against one of the mannequins, knocking it over. It fell to the floor with a crash, taking with it several others. The man in the doorway stepped forward and hoisted me up by the scruff of the neck. Claudia was screaming and kicking with her legs in the air but the man holding her was laughing. They dragged us through the battlefield of demolished dummies down the room towards the table. Bumbag was on his feet looking scared and surprised. I was half expecting him to recognize me but he didn't seem to. The others didn't move. I think they knew we were there all along. Granite Head still had his podgy hands on the

138

table and his eyelids drooped as he stared wearily at Claudia and me.

'Let me go!' yelled Claudia.

Granite Head nodded and the man holding Claudia released his grip. Claudia turned round and glared at him. For a moment I thought she was going to kick him. But then Granite Head said something in Italian. He repeated the same sentence three times. Each time in a slower and angrier voice.

'We don't understand,' said Claudia. She was lying. I knew she spoke fluent Italian but they didn't. 'I'm American and he's English.'

Granite Head stared at her, then with a strong accent asked, 'What are you doing here?'

'Just looking,' I stammered. 'Just exploring.'

Granite Head said something to Bumbag, who shook his head. Then he spoke to the two men standing beside us. They dragged us over to the corner of the room where some boxes stood beneath the arms. One of them reached into an open box and pulled out a handful of thin plastic ties, the kind you thread like a belt with little plastic teeth that clamp shut when you pull them tight.

They pulled our arms behind our backs, tied our wrists, then pushed us down onto the floor and tied our ankles. Bumbag was the only one who looked concerned. It sounded like he was pleading with Granite Head, but Granite Head took no notice. He pushed back his chair and with some difficulty stood up. The two on either side of him did the same. The one I thought might have been Big Baldy picked up the leg from the centre of the table and tucked it under his enormous arm. All six walked past us as we lay on the floor, trussed up like oven-ready chickens, but only Bumbag bothered to look down. He was staring at me and I was waiting for the penny to drop.

'Panettone!' laughed one of the others, holding up the blue box that Claudia had dropped on the floor.

'That's mine!' shouted Claudia. 'It's a present.'

'I do not think you will be giving any presents tonight,' grumbled Granite Head ominously. Then he nodded in the general direction of the table. The man holding the panettone shrugged his shoulders as if he couldn't see the sense in passing up the chance of free cake and placed it with dramatic reluctance in the centre of the table. They filed out of the door, switched off the light and left.

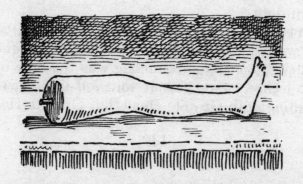

17

Arm over Arm

'We should never have come up here,' said Claudia accusingly.

'But we did.'

'Thanks to you!'

'*And you!* You were the first one up the stairs!'

'It was your idea.'

'It was ours.'

'You're the one who found that stupid head,' she added bitterly.

'Thanks a bunch.'

'My wrists hurt,' she whimpered.

'Mine too.'

'Where do you think they've gone?' she asked.

'You're the psychic one. You tell me.'

Claudia looked hurt.

'I'm sorry,' I said. Did you understand what they were talking about?'

'Money. Your friend Bumbag owes them money.'

'He's not my friend.'

'Do you think he recognized you?'

'I'm not sure. I don't think so.'

'If he does we've had it. We've probably had it anyway. I know they don't believe us and if they find out we know about the smuggling it'll be us they'll be stuffing inside the dummies.'

I looked across at the legs dangling in the shadows. She was right. We had to get out of here. I struggled to my feet and began hopping across the room.

'Where are you going?' asked Claudia nervously,

'I'm looking for something.'

'What?'

'Something sharp to cut these plastic ties.'

The dummies I'd knocked over lay where they'd fallen on the floor. One of the heads was split open and I remembered from opening up Angelina's head that the broken fibreglass left a sharp edge. I sat down beside it and positioned my wrists so that the plastic tie was against the split in the head and then I began sawing. It took ages but eventually it broke in two and my hands were free. I picked up the head and began on my feet. Claudia had joined me and was trying to do the same. When I broke free I helped her.

'What now?' she asked, rubbing her wrists, which were red and sore.

'Try the door,' I said.

'It's locked,' she answered, without touching the handle.

'It would be,' I agreed, but tried it anyway. It was.

'The windows?' I suggested.

'We're five floors up,' protested Claudia.

'We can shout for help,' I said.

We ran over to the windows and tried to open them but they wouldn't budge and the alley below looked as deserted as ever. Then we heard voices laughing and singing. There was someone down there, probably setting off to find a party. I grabbed a fibreglass arm from the wall and smashed the glass in one of the windows. The cold night air rushed in and the broken fragments of glass tinkled as they hit the pavement.

'*Ai!*' shouted a voice from below.

'*Help!*' we both shouted as horns started honking and several fireworks exploded nearby.

'*Help!*' we kept shouting, but whoever was below us was now running down the alley. Outside it sounded as though World War Three had started.

'It's no use,' said Claudia despondently. 'The party's already started. Bottles will be smashing in the streets and everyone will be yelling at the top of their voices. No one will hear us.'

'Then we need to get a message to someone – anyone. Something that lets them know we're here and in real trouble.'

'How?' she asked.

'How do you think?' I snapped back. 'Find something to write with!'

We switched the light back on and began searching the room. Claudia looked in the drawer of the table where Granite Head had sat and found a large red marker pen.

'We can use this to write with, but what are we going to write on?' she asked.

'There's got to be some paper here somewhere.'

'There's the cardboard boxes – we could tear one up.'

I walked over to a cardboard box and began ripping the top open, tearing off a large flap. Inside were some more plastic ties like the ones they'd used to tie our hands and wrists. I gave the piece of cardboard to Claudia.

'What should I say?'

'Say we've been kidnapped.'

'No one will take that seriously,' said Claudia cynically.

'Write down your name and your dad's telephone number, then maybe they will.'

When she'd finished we walked over to the broken window. Holding the message between my finger and thumb I stretched my arm out as far as I could then let go. We watched as it fell like a wounded bird and landed face down in a black puddle of rainwater.

'Great!' said Claudia sarcastically.

We sat on the floor staring into the room. Getting a message out was still our best hope. There had to be a way.

'We need some rope,' I said.

'No way!' insisted Claudia. 'Forget it. I'm not climbing down there.'

'Not to climb down. We need some rope or string or something to lower one of those out of the window,' I said, pointing at the legs. 'We can write the message on it.'

While Claudia rewrote the message on the leg I searched the room again but couldn't find anything resembling a coil of rope. And then I remembered the box of plastic ties. When they were undone each was about half a metre long. I began fastening them together.

'That's going to take for ever,' moaned Claudia. 'We're five storeys up, remember. Besides, there's not nearly enough of them.'

'Have you got a better idea?' I snapped back.

'The other legs?' suggested Claudia.

'What?'

'The other legs ... We could tie them all together and lower them out of the window.'

It was a good idea. We set to work. There were two kinds of leg. One standard leg shape and one that incorporated the hips. We used the legs with the hips so that we had something to fasten the plastic ties to and began lowering them out of the broken window, tying them hip to hip and foot to foot, one at a time. About half an hour later the legs ran out and we were still about five metres short of the pavement. We'd used twelve altogether. Altogether they weighed a ton and the plastic ties were being strained to breaking point. I attached them to a nail that was hammered into the window frame.

'If someone sees them they're bound to think something's up,' I said hopefully.

'Like what?' said Claudia, obviously not convinced.

'It can't be every window in Florence that's got a chain of legs dangling from it,' I said.

'It's New Year's Eve,' said Claudia, sliding her back down the wall and placing her head in her hands.

All we could do was sit and wait, hoping someone would see the legs and be curious enough to find a ladder and read the message. It seemed hopeless. We must have sat there for hours with only the faceless dummies for company. We were cold and scared, our ears tuned to the click of a lock and the ominous plod of footsteps on the stairs.

'We could try flicking the light off and on. Send an SOS,' I suggested.

Claudia shivered and gave me a withering

146

look. We both lapsed into a silence punctuated by the distant explosions of fireworks and what sounded like a piano playing a long way off.

'What's the time?' I asked eventually.

'Ten past ten,' said Claudia, glancing at her watch. 'Dad and Dot will be really worried.'

'Maybe they'll have told the police. Maybe they're looking for us,' I suggested as a silvery glow suddenly spread over the dummies at the other end of the room.

'What's that?' asked Claudia, grabbing my arm.

It was the moon shining through a small window we hadn't noticed at the other end of the building. We ran through the dummies and climbed some boxes so that we could look out. About four metres below us a tiled rooftop stretched out towards a roof garden and what looked like a penthouse with lights shining inside. I tried the handle of the window and it opened. When I stuck my head out I could see a wooden ladder but it was lying far away against the wall of the roof garden. I looked down at the tiled roof below the window. The slope was quite gentle and four metres wasn't that high.

'You can't jump!' insisted Claudia. 'You'd be jumping onto tiles. They'd probably crack and fall and you'd go with them.'

She was right.

'The arms,' I said. 'We'll tie the arms together and I'll climb down them.'

147

'You're mad.'

'Then we just sit here and wait for the Cammisas?'

We tied the arms together and lowered them out of the little window until the fingers of the first one were stroking the tiles. Then we anchored them inside by tying them to a leg and wedging it across the window frame.

'Be careful!' urged Claudia.

'I'll try,' I replied, backing out of the window with a firm grip round the wrist of a fibreglass arm.

My legs were dangling in space, scrabbling against the wall. The arms began flailing about, rattling against the brickwork. I held my breath, let go with one hand and grabbed the next wrist. When I looked back up I could see Claudia's face leaning out of the window, tense with concern. And when I looked down I could see the orange tiles sloping gently away to the edge of the roof and a yawning gap of black space. Nine arms later my feet touched the tiles, which shifted slightly under my weight.

'You *next*!' I shouted.

'I can't.'

'You have to,' I said.

'I'm afraid of heights. I can't do it. You go and get help.'

'What if they come back?'

'I can't do it,' she sobbed.

Then I remembered the ladder.

'Wait. I'll fetch that ladder. Could you do it then?'

'I think so.'

I turned and set off across the rooftop with one foot on either side of the ridge and my arms held out sideways for balance. It had stopped raining but the tiles were wet and slippery and there was a wind blowing. All around me lights shone from top-floor windows and the black night sky erupted with cascades of coloured sparks. I concentrated on my feet, taking one small step at a time.

When I reached the roof garden I could smell the herbs that were growing there and I thought I could hear voices from inside the penthouse beyond it. My instinct was to jump over the wall and bang against the penthouse door, but then I turned round and saw Claudia's head still framed in the window. I grabbed the ladder, knocking a plant pot off the wall which smashed to pieces on the roof.

I set off back along the ridge, dragging the ladder behind me. When I arrived at the other end I propped it against the wall but it wasn't quite long enough to reach the window. Claudia would have to lower herself arm over arm for the first metre or so.

'Come on!' I urged.

'I can't,' she sobbed.

'Yes you can. You have to!'

149

'What about the head?'

'Leave it!'

Tentatively she backed out until her feet were touching the topmost rung of the ladder.

'You've done it,' I said. 'Now just step down. Don't look round. Keep a grip on the arms. One at a time.'

I watched her, steadying the ladder until she was standing beside me. She turned round. Her hair was blowing in the wind. Her moonlit face was white and scared and she looked exactly like Bernini's Daphne. I thought it was just her fear of heights, but then I noticed she was looking straight ahead over my shoulder. I turned round and saw two men on the roof walking slowly along the ridge towards us. They were the same two that had grabbed us in the factory. The others, including Granite Head and Bumbag, were standing at the edge of the roof garden watching their progress. That's where they'd disappeared to. That's who I'd heard talking in the penthouse and who'd heard me smashing the flowerpot on the roof.

There was nowhere to run. We just waited while they approached. They said nothing, simply pointed back up at the open window. I went first so I could help Claudia back inside. She was crying. I guessed that being psychic when things are going from bad to worse wasn't much help.

18

The Proof in the Pudding

They made us sit at the table at the far end of
the big room beneath the cold blue fluorescent
light that shone directly onto the pale blue
panettone box, waiting to explode like a time
bomb. There was a draught of cold air blowing
through the broken windowpane and it wasn't
long before one of them noticed. When he saw
the legs dangling down he looked totally
gobsmacked. He called for his mate to come over:
they said something to each other, burst out
laughing then started to haul them back in
through the window. I was waiting for them to
find the message on the last leg, but the last leg
didn't appear. When I tried to count them I could
only make out eleven and I was sure we'd used
twelve, but when I tried to count them again
there seemed to be thirteen.

'My dad and your Auntie Dot will be seriously scared by now,' said Claudia, sniffing back some tears.

'Yes, they will be,' I agreed, thinking, *So am I*, but not wanting to say it. There was still a chance that Bumbag hadn't recognized me. If he hadn't, then as far as they were concerned we were just two kids who'd stumbled into something they knew nothing about. All they needed to do was give us a good scare and send us packing – hopefully with our panettone box, but to tell the truth I didn't really care any more. All I wanted was to get out of there in one piece.

Acting scared wasn't a problem, especially when we heard the heavy plodding footsteps coming up the stairs. The door swung open and in walked Granite Head followed by Bumbag, Big Baldy and Big Baldy's brother. Granite Head didn't look too pleased. He didn't like climbing stairs and we were the reason he'd had to climb them for a second time that night. He half sighed and half snarled at us, his flabby jowls trembling and his flabby eyelids almost covering his eyes.

In complete contrast Bumbag looked positively elated. He had a smile on his face that split his head from ear to ear but it wasn't the kind of smile that was meant to relax you. It was the kind that vampires wear before they sink their teeth into their victim's neck. Judging by the way his eyes were fixed on me, I was the one he was after. The penny had obviously dropped and so had any hopes of being sent packing. He strode towards us, his expensive leather shoes clattering on the wooden floor. I could hear him breathing slowly and deeply through his pointy nose. He was standing trembling with agitation at the edge of the table with nothing but the blue panettone box between me and him.

'It's you,' he said, pointing a rigid forefinger at my head. 'I *knew* I'd seen you before.'

I tried to look confused. 'I d-don't know what you mean,' I stammered.

'It was you on the island of Skye. You who found the head. I want that head.'

'*What head?* I don't know what you're talking about.'

'Don't play games with me, boy,' he snapped, stabbing the air with his finger. 'You know what I want. You know what was inside. Where is it?'

I didn't know what to say. All the others, including old Granite Head, were standing behind him like ugly dummies selling black suits. If I gave him the head we were probably done for. I couldn't see how they'd let us go. There was no way they'd trust us to keep quiet. The last hour of the year was ticking away. Outside fireworks were exploding and car horns honking. Everyone else in Florence was celebrating. I wanted to be a million miles away.

I wanted this to be a dream so that I could change the ending.

'It was a cabbage,' I said.

Bumbag looked confused. 'What are you talking about?' he demanded.

'That's what was in the sack the day you chased me on Skye.'

'Do you take me for a complete fool?' he shouted, slamming the tabletop with his fist so that the panettone box jumped.

'I didn't know what you wanted. I was scared. I heard you smashing up the shed and just ran.'

Bumbag's eyes creased to narrow slits as the muscles in his bony face tightened. He was having trouble believing this. Granite Head staggered forward and asked him a question. Bumbag replied and Granite Head curled his flabby lip and snorted something to his henchmen. One grabbed me and the other grabbed Claudia.

'Regrettably you leave us no alternative,' said Bumbag calmly. 'It is now your heads that will go missing.'

He looked from me to Claudia, then back to me, but there wasn't a hint of regret on his face.

The air in the room seemed suddenly to disappear. I was fighting for breath.

'*Polizia!*' A loud megaphoned voice echoed from the street below. The Cammisas and Bumbag all rushed to the window like flies trying to escape. At the end of the room the door was flung open and four armed policemen rushed in. They crouched at the end of the room amongst the naked dummies with machine guns pointed at the Cammisas. Old Granite Head swayed to one side, someone shouted something and he froze.

Moments later a tall man sauntered through the door wearing a grey woollen overcoat, a grey felt hat and brown leather gloves. Bumbag tried to speak but one of the armed policemen told him to shut up. The tall man paused and slowly surveyed the room with the armed policemen, the dummies, the Cammisas, Bumbag and us. Finger by finger he removed his brown leather gloves and put them in the pocket of his overcoat. No one uttered a sound. Then he walked slowly towards us, removing his hat and placing it on the head of one of the dummies.

'*Polizia*,' he said, producing a small black wallet and flicking it open. 'Ispettore Cappelli.'

He looked at Claudia and said something in Italian. Claudia took my arm and we stepped out from behind the table, walking across the room until we were beside him. Granite Head started swaying again. His eyelids had closed almost completely and it looked like he was ready to collapse. He fell back against the table clutching at his chest as all four machine guns swerved in his direction. The man in the overcoat said something. The armed policemen surrounded the table and one by one all the men sat down.

'They were going to kill us,' said Claudia.

The man in the overcoat nodded and said something to Bumbag. Bumbag started babbling on, pointing at us, pointing at the dummies and pointing at the broken window.

'What's he saying?' I asked Claudia.

'He's saying we're a couple of vandals. He says they caught us smashing the place up and they were just giving us a scare before they called the police.'

'Tell him!' I said.

Claudia said something and then the detective turned to me. He spoke slowly in English.

'Your friend says you have proof that these men are criminals.'

'Yes.'

Bumbag rose to his feet but one of the other policemen pushed him back into his chair. He was babbling on again, trying to sound relaxed, laughing nervously as if he'd just told a bad joke.

'What's he saying?' I asked Claudia.

'He's telling the detective who he is. He says he's here on museum business and that he can't possibly believe our word against his.'

'Show me the proof,' said the detective, turning back to me.

'It's in the panettone box,' I said.

Everyone's eyes were fixed on the box. The detective walked towards the table, leant across and placed his finger under the plastic handle. He lifted it up and let it dangle there as if testing its weight. Bumbag turned white as the blood drained from his face. The detective set the box back down on the table, opened it and pulled out ... a dome-shaped, golden-coloured cake studded with currants.

'Happy New Year!' he said. 'You are all under arrest.'

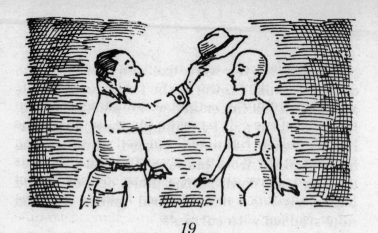

19

Falling into Place

We left the building escorted by the detective, who retrieved his grey felt hat from the obliging dummy and held open the door. Bumbag and his associates were obviously not coming with us. They were still surrounded by the four armed policemen, who were waiting for reinforcements, and were under strict instructions to remain seated with their hands clearly visible on the tabletop. It was a strange sight. They were all staring at the cake, which remained on display, as if waiting for permission to eat it. But this wasn't much of a party. It was more like Bumbag's Last Supper.

'I don't understand,' I said, still reeling from the shock of being rescued in possession of a panettone. 'I thought the Bernini—'

But the detective held up a gloved hand and as

we descended the stairs he began to explain.

Our box with Bernini's head of Daphne wrapped snugly in cotton wool had been left on the floor of the café opposite the museum. In the rush to follow Bumbag I'd picked up the wrong box. When the family who were sitting next to us got up to leave they were puzzled that one of their panettones seemed much heavier than the other, so they opened it up and had no trouble recognizing what was inside. Pictures of the missing carving had been on the front page of every newspaper. They took it straight to the police station and gave them a vague description of the two most wanted art thieves in Italy.

Auntie Dot had had a bad day. She'd felt some seriously bad vibes standing in front of a painting called *The Massacre of the Innocents* – apparently the details were fairly graphic. She'd left the museum just before we arrived and had walked back alone in the rain, convinced that something awful had happened. The streets seemed full of impatient gas-guzzling cars, the pavements seething with real fur coats and the shop windows positively oozing with extravagance and blood. By the time she arrived at the tower her unshakeable karma had been knocked sideways. The professor had poured her a glass of wine and endeavoured to reassure her that we were OK, but after a couple of hours her obvious unease became contagious and he'd decided to call the police, giving them a detailed description – which matched the one they already had.

We paused on the second-floor landing and stood aside as six armed policemen – the reinforcements – went up the stairs.

'But how did you find us?' asked Claudia.

The detective smiled but said nothing, and knocked on the door behind him. A smartly dressed lady with dark brown eyes and bright red lips opened it.

'This is Signora Bertolli.'

The lady turned her eyes to us and smiled.

'Signora Bertolli is a piano teacher. It was she who found your message.'

Signora Bertolli nodded. 'I am so relieved you are safe,' she said. 'I must admit, it gave me quite a shock. I had just finished playing my piano when I heard a funny noise. I went through to my living room and I saw a leg dangling in front of the window with its toes tapping at the glass. You can imagine my surprise. I thought it was some sort of joke, but then I noticed the writing on the leg so I took a knife from my kitchen, opened the window and cut the leg free. When I read the message I rang Professor Mason.'

'And he rang us,' added the detective. 'The rest . . .' He shrugged his shoulders and tugged his felt hat. 'There are still many questions that

160

need answering. Not least being how you came to be in possession of the carving in the first place. But I think you have both had enough to deal with for one night and those questions can wait until –' he glanced at his wrist watch – 'next year.'

The detective was right, our ordeal had taken its toll. I looked at Claudia. Her eyes were wide, brown and unblinking but instead of being certain and intense they were wary and scared. I knew mine must have looked the same. I wanted to sleep. I wanted my mum.

When we stepped outside the alley was no longer dark. There were four police cars, two at either end, shining their headlights on the doorway of Fratelli Cammisa, and parked alongside one of the police cars I recognized the less impressive but no less welcome sight of Bessie.

Standing beside her was the professor, wearing an ancient blue duffel coat, and standing next to him was Auntie Dot and a smartly dressed police woman. Auntie Dot was wearing a blanket. When they saw us she and the professor both rushed forward. Her blanket dropped to the ground. I started running. So did Claudia. The professor met her halfway, lifted her up and swung her round. I slowed down; so did Auntie Dot. She'd been crying – I could see her cheeks were wet with tears and her glasses were all steamed up. I ran across and grabbed her, pressing my face against hers, feeling her hand on the back of my head pressing me harder. For the first time in ages I felt safe.

20

A Birthday Surprise

It was the smell of bacon cooking that eventually woke me up. I thought I was back home, but it was New Year's Day and I was still in Florence. I'd slept through the bells – a bottomless, black, velvety sleep, the kind that wraps itself round you so that you seem to disappear. There are no dreams in that kind of sleep, no reminders, just rest.

The sunlight shone accusingly through the windows, glinting on the necks of empty wine bottles and dirty dishes smeared red with pasta sauce. I could hear a trickle of water behind me and turned to see the professor watering the plants.

'Good morning,' he said, looking particularly bright eyed and fresh as though he'd been up and about for hours.

'What time is it?' I yawned.

'Ten o'clock.'

'Is everyone else up?'

'Claudia's awake but still in bed. Dorothy's cooking your breakfast.'

'Bacon?' I said in disbelief.

'Bacon,' confirmed the professor, raising his white eyebrows and nodding sagely.

This was worrying. The traumas of yesterday had obviously done her head in. I threw back the green duvet and clambered down the spiral staircase wondering how I was going to break the news to Dad that Auntie Dot had flipped. She was standing in the kitchen some distance from the sizzling pan, prodding at the rashers with a long wooden spatula that she held at arm's length.

'Are you all right?' I asked cautiously.

'I'm fine. Really, really fine. And how are you?'

'Fine.'

'I just thought you'd like some breakfast.'

'Bacon?'

'Yes.'

'For me?'

'Well, it's certainly not for me,' she insisted.

'But I thought . . .'

'Thought what?'

'Thought it was against your principles.'

'It is really, but I've decided that principles sometimes get in the way.'

'Of what?'

'Of being a friend,' she said, lifting the almost black, shrivelled rashers from the pan and flipping them onto two slices of white bread.

I took a bite and smiled appreciatively.

Auntie Dot looked concerned. 'I've cremated it, haven't I?'

'No, it's good, kind of . . . well done!' I said through a mouthful of bacon-flavoured charcoal.

'I'll have to learn how to do it properly,' she said, obviously not fooled.

'Dad can give you lessons,' I said.

Around midday the four of us went to the police station to meet Detective Cappelli and fill in the gaps surrounding the disappearance and recovery of the Bernini carving. I'd been dreading this, but somehow the tall, cool policeman with his grey hat, grey coat and brown leather gloves seemed like someone I could talk to.

I'd been thinking about what I was going to tell him – thinking about Roddy and how he'd died. Maybe because of that head and maybe not. I thought about his sister Katie, alone in their croft, happy that her brother was resting safely in the consecrated ground of the little church. I thought about Glen, about the peat tea, the grandfather clock and the little green hut, now abandoned and left for the fairies. I didn't want that ending to change.

I told Detective Cappelli about the Isle of

Skye, about finding the dummies washed up on the beach and how I'd decided to keep one of the heads for a souvenir and how I'd been chased by Bumbag but had got away. I also had to explain why I hadn't gone to the police when I discovered the Bernini carving inside. Why I'd kept it secret. That was hard because it meant talking about Mum.

He seemed to understand. He said there'd be a trial and that we might both be required to give evidence but that would be some way off. He also said we had become celebrities. The recovery of the Bernini carving was major news and apparently there were as many journalists after our story as there were days left in the year. The front pages of the newspapers were illustrated with artists' impressions of Claudia and me dangling from a chain of artificial limbs hundreds of feet above the streets of Florence. Alongside this were three photographs – one of Bernini's head of Daphne; another of Signor Balla, director of the City Museum, who was implicated in its theft and under arrest; and another of a smiling Signora Bertolli cradling in her arms the last leg, on which we had scrawled our desperate message.

Neither of us relished the prospect of being bombarded with more questions. The professor brought Bessie round to the back of the police station and we made a dash for it.

'I hope you don't mind accompanying me on a little visit I make every year,' said the professor, as we drove north, leaving the city behind and heading towards the pale blue hills. 'We're going to meet a very special lady,' he went on, glancing over his shoulder at Claudia and me as Auntie Dot gripped the dashboard and tried to look calm. 'Signora Amalfi. She was my secretary at the university for over twenty years. She retired a long time ago but we still keep in touch and I always go to see her on her birthday, which is today. She used to live across the piazza from the tower but now she has moved back to the little village where she was born. To the farm that her parents left her. She is eighty-one and she lives all alone.'

We sat back and watched as the buildings shrank and the hills grew, unfurling in a gentle swirl of greys, browns and greens. Signora Amalfi's village sat astride one of these hills, a cubist clutter of creamy-coloured walls and terracotta roofs. The farm was at the very edge, perched on the crest of a hill which overlooked a valley of vineyards and olive groves. Bessie made a dramatic entrance, swerving into the farmyard in a cloud of brown dust, white feathers and indignant, squawking chickens. Claudia felt a bit sick after the winding roads so the professor suggested we went for some fresh air while he and Auntie Dot went inside. We could join them all later. There would be a little party, but not until tea time.

Claudia and I walked out of the yard and round the back of a barn from where you could see the whole valley. The air smelt of fresh herbs and wood smoke. The sky was a brilliant blue and already in the west it was softening to something paler and tinged with the creamy orange light of a late winter afternoon.

'You'll be going back soon,' said Claudia.

'Day after tomorrow.'

'Your dad is missing you.'

'I know.'

'You should call him and wish him a happy new year.'

'I will.'

'Does he know about the head and everything?'

'Don't think so. Auntie Dot said we shouldn't tell him until we get back. She said he'd only get worked up about it and start worrying.'

'She's probably right.'

'Probably,' I agreed.

'I like your Auntie Dot. She feels things.'

'How'd you mean?'

'Well, not exactly *psychic*, but really sensitive.'

'She's a Buddhist,' I said, but Claudia didn't reply. She didn't seem interested. She was staring over my shoulder in the direction of the barn. I looked round but all I could see was the big open door and the shadows inside.

'Did you see him?' she asked.

'Who?'

'That man.'

'*What man?*'

'He was wearing what looked like an old army uniform and he had a handful of eggs. He was smiling at us.'

'So?'

'Nothing,' said Claudia. 'I just thought Dad said that Signora Amalfi lived by herself.'

'Perhaps he helps her out? Where did he go?'

'He was standing just inside the barn.'

I walked over to the barn door and peered inside but there was no sign of life. Claudia was gazing out across the valley, watching a flock of starlings chattering in the treetops, ready to head south to the city.

'Dad and Auntie Dot are—'

'I know,' she interrupted.

This was like talking to yourself.

'And you didn't like it at first, but it's getting easier, isn't it?'

I didn't say anything. There didn't seem much point.

'Claudia! Claude!' shouted the professor.

We walked back into the yard and over to the farmhouse. Inside it was much darker. There were no electric lights – just the orangey glow from an open fire flickering on a row of copper pans and hand-painted plates that hung on the wall. Bunches of dried flowers hung from the ceiling and sitting in an armchair by the fire was an old lady with white hair tied back in a bun. She smiled when we walked in.

'Claudia, Claude, this is Signora Amalfi,' said the professor.

'Pleased to meet you,' we both said.

'I have heard so much about you,' she replied. 'I no longer read the newspapers but Ricardo has told me of your adventures and how you found the missing head of Daphne.'

'In Scotland,' I said; 'on an island called Skye.'

'Ahhh . . . the *misty* isle . . .' she whispered, turning towards the fire.

'Have you been there?' I asked in surprise as the professor's mobile phone suddenly started playing 'Auld Lang Syne'.

'Excuse me,' he said, stepping to one side. 'Hello! Yes . . . Yes . . . And to you too . . . Indeed they are. They're here right now. I'll put them on. It's your dad,' he said, handing me the phone. 'I think you'll get a better signal outside.'

Auntie Dot followed me out into the yard. The sun was setting and the crumbling stone walls of the farm buildings were glowing like polished gold.

'*Hello?*' said Dad.

'Dad, it's me. Happy New Year!'

'*And you too. How's things?*'

'Great!'

'You're having a good time?'

'Fantastic!'

'And Auntie Dot?'

'I'll put her on.'

Auntie Dot took a step backwards, gesturing for me to talk for a little longer. From inside the farm, Claudia shouted my name.

'What was that?' asked Dad.

'It's Claudia,' I said.

'It's cloudier here too,' said Dad. *'There's been a deep depression centred over the Azores since New Year's Eve, causing an occluded front with its associated blanket of stratocumulus.'*

I held the phone out to Auntie Dot. I couldn't speak for laughing. Some things never change.

'What's so funny? What's he talking about?' she asked.

'One guess,' I said.

Then something special happened, something I hadn't seen before. Auntie Dot made the same face that Mum used to make – the same look of pretend surprise that had been on the face of Bernini's Daphne.

'Dad,' I said, holding the phone back to the side of my head, 'I'm putting Auntie Dot on, but don't talk about the weather. Talk about us – us three.'

'Claude!' shouted Claudia.

I handed the phone to Dot and went inside.

'Dad's lit the candles,' she whispered as I came through the door.

Signora Amalfi sat by the fire. A door swung open and in marched the professor carrying a panettone bedecked with eighty-one tiny party candles.

'*Happy birthday to you . . .*' he began, '*Happy birthday to you . . . Happy birthday, Angelinaaa . . .*'

THE END